Where in the World is Xavier Cockroachal Damon?

Aaron Aaronson

Published by Aaron Aaronson, 2022.

This is a work of fiction. Similarities to real people, places, or events are entirely coincidental.

WHERE IN THE WORLD IS XAVIER COCKROACHAL DAMON?

First edition. October 20, 2022.

Copyright © 2022 Aaron Aaronson.

ISBN: 979-8223321491

Written by Aaron Aaronson.

I have a story I want to tell.

It is different from the stories I have written in the past. You see, I, myself have never appeared as a character in any of the stories I have penned. Certainly, many of the characters were indeed direct representations of myself and my life, but they were always just that, fictionalized representations rather than presenting real events as they actually happened. With this story it is different, for in it I will merely detail events of my life that recently happened and present the words and actions exactly as they occurred. It was a quite interesting adventure that would lend some credence to the old adage, truth is stranger than fiction. There are events in life that make you reassess everything you thought you knew, that change the person you are, and after these events, you see the world, life, everything differently. The events I will now detail would certainly represent that assertion. So, if you're interested in hearing the story, continue on and, who knows, you may actually be surprised at what you read.

I sat on my bed in my room. I was smoking a cigarette and drinking from a glass of vodka. I was trying to figure out what to do with the day. I couldn't think of anything. I was just blocked. In the past, ideas came so freely and once they did, I would sail along with them as if in a canoe, speeding down a rapid stream and the words would flow so freely until reaching that two word phrase that sealed the process, the end. It was just that lately, I couldn't find the words, any words that had meaning, or even any words that seemed worthy of commiting to paper for any reason. My soul felt like it was in lockdown and I could come up with absolutely no reason to write a single word, alone in my cell. Nothing seemed to matter. There didn't seem a point or purpose to anything and commentary on life or the world seemed an utter waste of time. I felt I had already said all there was to say and saying anything more would be nothing more than peeling open old wounds to let the words bleed out. But, they would just be the same damn words, with minor tweaks or alterations, bleeding from the same damn wound of life. And the blood had all run dry, frozen and dead inside. I felt entirely lacking in any inspiration to say anything whatsoever and, to be honest, I really just wished all of the words of the world to burn and forever remain as ashes so that not a single one could ever be transcribed to paper again because I could think of not a single reason that a single word should ever grace a page again in some utter charade of absolute meaninglessness and nauseatingly insignificant pointlessness, screaming or whispering to the stale, dead air, with no one hearing a word, and it mattering not at all if they even did because commiting words to paper was without a doubt the purest depiction of the disgusting, cruel folly that is the futile, nothingness that is life.

As I said, I was blocked. I sat there searching my mind for anything worth writing, a new project I could embark upon, and all I saw was nothing, just dead words you could set into their tomb upon the page but not worthy of any stage to have themselves spoken upon. I needed something, some inspiration, something to light a spark, but what? I racked my brain but saw no answers. I finished the drink in my glass and filled another and from the glass I sipped.

The doorbell of my apartment rang.

My cigarette was at its end so I put it out in the ashtray. I set my glass down on my nightstand and I got up from the bed and gripped my cane, which had been standing next to the bed. I walked with my cane over to the door and answered it. Standing there was a man. He wore an old time bellhop outfit and a round, brimless, bellhop cap. The outfit was red with gold trimming. He had a long, thin, black mustache.

"Um, yes, can I help you?" I asked with confusion.

The man enthusiastically responded, "Why, it is my job to help you. That is what I am here for and I am here to inform you that you have received a telegram."

I looked at him with a perplexed look, scrunching my face. "A telegram? Is this a joke? Why the hell would someone send me a telegram?"

"Why, that I cannot say. I, of course, haven't read it, though I assure you this isn't a joke and it arrived at the front desk just a few minutes ago and I was instructed to come up to your room and deliver it promptly." He spoke with a dutiful quality.

My confusion was only greatly increased. "What are you talking about? What front desk? This is a cheap, rundown, should probably be condemned, apartment building. There is no front desk. And come up to my room. You do realize I am on the first floor?"

"Well, we aim to please and want to make sure all our guests at our lovely hotel are satisfied with the service." he cordially replied.

"This isn't a damn hotel. It's my apartment." I snapped with somewhat anger. "And who the hell would send a telegram? I really don't think they even still exist?"

The man spoke with an uncertain voice, "Oh, sir, I cannot tell you who sent it for that is information it is not for me to know. The front desk merely instructed me to deliver it to you."

"Again, this isn't a damn hotel and there is no front desk. Who the hell are you?" I questioned.

The man smiled graciously. "I am merely an employee of the hotel, here to serve your needs, and I was tasked with delivering to you a telegram."

I looked at him with doubt. "Really, a telegram. Well then give me the telegram."

"Indeed, sir, here you are." The man pulled out an envelope and handed it to me. "If there is anything else I can do for you, just call down to the front desk. I hope you enjoy your stay here. You have a wonderful day." The man turned and walked away and I closed the door.

OK, that wasn't at all weird.

Who the hell had that person been? I wondered to myself. Why did he keep claiming this was a hotel? I then realized that when I woke up, I hadn't actually taken notice of my surroundings, just sat up from the bed and lit a cigarette and poured myself a drink, so it was possible I had been out on an all night binge and had actually ended up checking into a hotel and it was me that was mistaken. I quickly darted my gaze around and scanned the room. No, no doubt about it, this was my crappy, shithole apartment. So then, who was that person? Why was he dressed like that? And why would he give me a telegram? I looked down at the telegram I held in my hand. It was a large envelope. My name was listed as the recipient. There was no indication who the sender was. But, a telegram? To have received it really didn't make any sense. I mean, it was 2051. Telegrams were such a bygone, forgotten relic that they had, I assumed, certainly been cast into the dustbin of history. By God, when was the last time anyone even heard mention of a telegram, thirty years ago or something maybe, when I was, like, seventeen. Even back then, if someone had asked if telegrams were still in use, no one would have had any idea. I, personally, had never once heard of them still being around as a means of communication at any point. But, now, in the year 2051, I stood there in my room, holding a telegram in my hand. It was all very, very strange.

I walked with my cane over to my bed. I sat down. I took a drink from my glass and pulled out and lit a cigarette. I opened the envelope that contained the telegram. What the telegram said was very peculiar. It said, "I am writing this to inform you that Hurphuldurp Mahangahoo is not actually dead. The body that was pulled from the rubble was a plant, a decoy. Hurphuldurp Mahangahoo lives. Also, a question for you. How do you know a cockroach is actually dead unless you see it dead with your own eyes. I suppose the same would be true for a Cockroachal. How do you know a Cockroachal is dead if the body was never found? Well, I suppose you could ask Hurphuldurp

Mahangahoo that question if you are able to find him. Follow the clues and you will find your answers."

I was flabbergasted at what I was reading. This was amazing. Hurphuldurp Mahangahoo, he was a character who died at the end of the story, "The Mystery of the Missing Dead". I thought he was just a fictional character, though, I never imagined he was actually a real person. And then the talk of a Cockroachal. Why that could only be referring to Xavier Cockroachal Damon, without a doubt the absolute greatest writer of all time, the most amazing, talented writer of this or any generation, the most genius, important, mind bogglingly extraordinary writer in history, a maestro of the written word that no other writer could possibly dream of ever even thinking of holding a candle to in terms of literary excellence. He was just that good. But, Xavier Cockroachal Damon had died at the end of his autobiography when he fell over a giant waterfall in his duel with the Ignonomous and Preposterous Hapheshalesh, who turned out to actually be Moriarty in disguise. I mean, everybody knew this, absolutely everybody. I think they even teach it in school, it's so well known. I was actually the one who wrote the introduction to "The Missing Years", which was added to his autobiography after his death. The Missing Years was written by Xavier Cockroachal Damon, detailing years not covered in his original published autobiography. It was discovered after his death and I felt very strongly it should be added and so I wrote the introduction because Xavier Cockroachal Damon was no longer around to do so.

But, the body was never recovered. He was just pronounced dead. Was the telegram suggesting that Xavier Cockroachal Damon was still alive? But then, how would Hurphuldurp Mahangahoo have that answer? Unless, was Hurphuldurp Mahangahoo actually Xavier Cockroachal Damon in disguise? Now that I think back to the story, that actually seems entirely plausible. That idea really was strongly suggested in a not so subtle way. But then, who sent this telegram to me, and why? Was it Xavier Cockroachal Damon, himself? No, that wouldn't make any sense. Why would he fake his own death, assume a new identity, to just fake his death again, to then reveal it all to me? No, the telegram had to have been sent by somebody else, but who? I felt dizzy. My head was spinning at the ramifications of what I had just read. I filled my glass and took a long gulp then pulled out and lit a cigarette then drank from my glass again.

Yes. Certainly, the logical and wise response when you feel dizzy and your head is spinning is to down vodka and light up a cigarette. But, I digress.

What was going on here? Who sent the telegram? Was Xavier Cockroachal Damon actually still alive? I had no answers but I was determined to get to the bottom of this and uncover the truth, so that was what I set out to do. I put my cigarette out in the ashtray. I grabbed my backpack and put it on. I stood from the bed and grabbed the handle of my cane. I walked across the room to my walker, my mode of transportation when outside. I unfolded it and opened the door and stepped outside, closing the door behind me.

I sat in a chair in my room, drinking from a glass of vodka and smoking a cigarette. It turns out that I had set out on my quest for answers, armed only with the knowledge that Xavier Cockroachal Damon and Hurphuldurp Mahangahoo may actually still be alive and that they may very well be one in the same person. What I didn't actually have was any information whatsoever or any means to go about finding them, him, whatever, you get the point. I had nothing to go on, nowhere to start, no possible idea where to go from there. I mean, I didn't even know what Xavier Cockroachal Damon looked like. I was quite familiar with his writing but he was very much a recluse in his life and there were actually no public photographs that existed of him so I had never even seen a picture of him. Sure, I could go wandering the streets, hoping by chance I might bump into him but I wouldn't even know him if I saw him. Determining his physical location would have to be achieved by other means, if he was even actually alive, that is. I had to figure out some course of action that could possibly be beneficial, so that was what I was attempting to do.

I was coming up with nothing. I mean, let's assume the chain of events was accurate. Xavier Cockroachal Damon faked his death and assumed the identity Hurphuldurp Mahangoo and then faked his death yet again. There was no chance he would just show up somewhere using the name Hurphuldurp Mahangahoo or Xavier Cockroachal Damon. This meant that to track him down I would have to be looking for someone with an entirely different name. I had nothing to work with and it was really getting me frustrated. I needed something, anything.

The doorbell of my apartment rang.

I put out my cigarette in the ashtray. I grabbed my cane and stood and used it to walk over to the door. I opened it. Standing outside was an elderly, gypsy woman, wearing a long flowing gown and an ornate vest. She had a piercing, severe stare and a quivering, unsettled expression upon her rigid, wrinkled face. She had long white hair. Her appearance was, to say the least, startling and striking. The gypsy woman just stood there without speaking, occasionally jerking her head awkwardly. I was rather taken aback and decided that finding out the nature of her presence at my door would be a wise action. "I'm sorry, can I help you?"

"Tell me, my son, would you like a psychic reading?" the woman asked with a mysterious tone.

"Um, no, not particularly." I declined.

"Why, it is very reasonably priced, only fifty dollars." she announced.

I shook my head. "I'm sorry, but, really, no thank you."

With a gleam in her eye, she attempted to persuade me, "Come now, son, what do you have to lose?"

"Um, fifty dollars." I answered.

She waved her arms with mystery. "Oh, but, my son, think of all you have to gain."

I shook my head again. "Really, sorry, not interested."

She held up her finger, alluringly. "Well, you should know, with every reading there is a special reward."

"Such as what?" I asked, curious.

"Everyone who pays for a reading gets a free scoop of ice cream." she proclaimed.

I nodded my head sarcastically. "Hmm, tempting, even taking into account I don't like ice cream, but still, I'm sorry, no."

"I could give you a test of my powers if you are skeptical. Go ahead, ask me any question and I will answer it." she bargained.

Intrigued, I responded, "Really. Well then, OK If you can answer this question, certainly I will pay the fifty dollars for the reading. Tell me, do you know the whereabouts of Hurphuldurp Mahangahoo and Xavier Cockroachal Damon?"

The expression on her face immediately snapped to anger and contempt. "What? Oh, come on, those are the stupidest names I've ever heard. You know, if you aren't a believer in psychic abilities that's one thing, but there's no need to mock me. Jesus Christ, you're an asshole."

"Well, in my defense, I wasn't actually mocking you. Those are actually real names of people I am trying to find." I explained.

"Oh, bullshit. Like you expect me to believe that." she snapped.

"I'm being serious." I tried to make clear.

She looked at me with pure disgust. "Yeah, right. You know, it isn't easy being a door to door gypsy fortune teller. Indeed, there is mockery that comes with the job but let me tell you, this really takes the cake."

"I'm sorry if I offended you. I assure you, I didn't mean to." I apologized.

She glared at me and then spoke with ominous foreboding. "You mock my powers but soon you will realize how wrong you were to do so for it will lead to terrible consequences. By doing so, you have offended the mystical forces that govern us all and because of that, I see a vision whereby their vengeance will come down upon you. In the near future, you will meet a woman, a goddess you will see her as, and the two of you will enter into a torrid affair. And, you will fall in love." she laughed then spoke with an omniscient voice, "But, love is never what it seems, now is it? And you will pay a very steep price for trusting in her."

"That's sort of cryptic, isn't it?" I responded, somewhat taken aback.

"It's my prophecy and it will come to be and when it does you will realize how much of an asshole you are. And as you suffer, you will realize you never should have doubted me and you were a fool and just should have paid me the fifty dollars for a reading." she snarled.

"Um, but I didn't give you the fifty dollars and, well, you sort of just warned me with your dark premonition so I could sort of, if I meet a mysterious woman, sort of just steer clear and not get involved. My point being, what then would have been the gain in paying you the fifty when I now already know to walk away? You see what I'm saying here?" I rationalized.

She laughed three, little, taunting chuckles. "Oh, but you won't walk away. You are going to walk head first into it. Even with every intuition telling you it is a mistake, still, you are going to walk straight into it and leave yourself completely exposed as an easy target and that will bring about your downfall and your end. And why? Because you are a fool and you will so want to believe with your pathetic, useless heart."

"OK, I think I'd say you might need some work on your people skills if you wish to make a sale in the future, but, still, I should get back to what I was doing and it was still a pleasure meeting you." I concluded, to end the bizarre conversation.

"Well, it wasn't a pleasure meeting you!" she growled then turned and stormed off and I closed the door.

OK, that was, I mean, perfectly normal.

And so, the freaky gypsy woman offering a free scoop of ice cream had failed to shed any light on the potential whereabouts of Xavier Cockroachal Damon, AKA Hurphuldurp Mahangahoo. So, I realized I was going to have to pursue other avenues. It had admittedly been an odd and unexpected encounter.

But, what? What would those avenues be? It dawned on me that to find the particular avenue that would lead to an answer, what I should do was traverse all the avenues of the city. I took a drink and nodded my head with certainty of the brilliance of my plan. I put my backpack on and I walked with my cane to my walker, opened the walker, then opened the door, then stepped outside, closing the door behind me.

Look, I am well aware, after the fact, that this was the most idiotically ill conceived plan in all of history. In my defense, though, let's be honest here, it is never a valid defense of anything, I was quite drunk when the plan was hatched. But, bear in mind, my plan was just to go out and wander all of the avenues of New York City on foot, hoping I would come across something. Bear in mind, also and even more so, I am on a walker. I am a cripple. Bear in mind another relevant aspect of this endeavour, I had absolutely no clue what I might possibly be looking for. I was just heading out as a stumbling drunk, hobbling on his walker, hoping against hope he would get lucky and find something useful, even though, lucky was something this particular person never actually was.

The whole episode went to complete crap. I did indeed set out in earnest, hobbling out of my room on my walker, but, I, as any non-idiot might have expected, didn't find a single damn thing of any use whatsoever. I walked for like, three damn hours, of course covering the same amount of ground someone not crippled could have done in thirty minutes. Meaning, essentially, I pretty much walked to the corner store. Then, of course, I had to walk the three hours back, becoming so despondent at the futility of the failed endeavour that, at some point, even though realizing in my condition with a disability it really was not wise or safe to get even more drunk while out walking, did indeed do just that. What happened after that? I really have no damn clue. I blacked out. I do know though, from awaking the next morning, I did, in fact, actually make it back home, realizing how much of a damn fool I was for not better listening to reason and taking into consideration the simple, unavoidable reality of my condition. Christ, maybe if I didn't lose my memory so damn much, I would be better able to remember who it was I actually am.

So, as I sat in my room, sipping from a glass of vodka and smoking a cigarette, I knew I had to regroup. I needed a new course of action. I needed a new plan. But, what? What should my next steps be? I tried to think of something but was utterly stymied, coming up with nothing.

The doorbell rang.

I put my cigarette out in the ashtray. I grabbed my cane and walked over to the door. I opened the door and saw that standing there was the same man from before, dressed as he had been before, in the bellhop outfit. "You, again. What do you want?"

"Why, hello there, sir, I just wanted to check with you to see how you are enjoying your stay at our lovely hotel?" he replied with a cheery voice.

"I am neither enjoying nor am I not enjoying my stay at your hotel because this is not your damn hotel. This is my damn apartment. Seriously, who the hell are you?" I responded with frustration.

"I am merely a member of the staff who is here to cater to your needs." the man explained, explaining nothing at all.

"Yeah, well I need you to get the hell out of here." I barked with agitation.

"Well, if that is what you wish, sir, by all means. But, first, I should inform you, I have a telegram for you that arrived at the front desk just a few minutes ago." responded the man.

I gave him a dubious look. "A telegram?"

"Yes, sir." he replied with a smile.

"That arrived at the front desk." I challenged him.

"Yes, sir." He smiled again.

"Of my apartment building that has no front desk." I pointed out.

The man smiled even wider. "At the front desk of our wonderful hotel."

"Give me the damn telegram." I growled.

"By all means, sir, here you are." The man handed me a large envelope. "Now, is there anything else I can do for you?"

I sneered at him. "Yes, get the hell out of here."

The man cheerily smiled. "Very well, sir. If there is anything else you need, do not hesitate to call down to the front desk." The man turned and walked away and I closed the door.

I stood and just looked at the closed door, shaking my head. What the hell was the deal with that person? Why was he so insistent that, contrary to reality, this was a hotel room? I couldn't fathom what was going on with that. But, he had given me another telegram. I looked down at the telegram in my hand. I wondered to myself what this one said. Only one way to find out. I walked with my cane over to my bed and sat down. I poured a drink and took a sip then pulled out and lit a cigarette. I opened the envelope and looked at the telegram contained inside. It said, "To solve the riddle you are faced with and uncover the whereabouts of the person you seek, you must find a street of berries, ah, but what street would that be? I guess that answer you have to Mull. If you are able to locate this street, use the numbers as your guide and ask yourself, what is half of 36 and then halve it again. If you are able to find the place, you will be faced with a conundrum. How can a man grow to three stories taller than where he currently stands? Solve this then 10 times 2 plus 2 plus 2 plus 4 plus 4. Do you know how to find the door? Good luck."

It was obviously directions but presented as a riddle that I had to solve. Um, a ludicrously simplistic riddle. I mean, I had to Mull how to find a street of berries. That would be Mulberry Street which was a couple miles away. Half of half of thirty-six. Um, nine. So go to nine Mulberry Street. How does a man grow to three stories taller than where he stands, gee, I don't know, maybe take the freakin elevator. And, um, I do know how to do rudimentary math, ten times two plus two plus two plus four plus four. Go to number thirty-two. So the answer was to go to nine Mulberry Street and go to room thirty-two. You know, didn't telegrams, when they were in use, charge by the number of words? The telegram could have just said that and saved a hell of a lot of money. Jesus Christ, was this thing written by a five year old with a large piggy bank and a head wound?

I put on my backpack and set out to go see what the nine Mulberry Street address was all about and how it pertained to my investigation. It was a couple miles away and being on a walker that meant that I had to take the bus. Man, how I fuckin hated taking the bus. It had nothing to do with any of the common complaints that led so many to abhor public transit. It was entirely because I was on a walker and I absolutely despised being a, "Can someone please move to give him a seat" person. If, when it approached, I saw that the bus was full and there were no open seats up front I would merely walk away and await the next bus to see if hopefully it was less crowded. I stood there at the bus stop, smoking a cigarette. The bus approached, there were several open seats. I flicked away my cigarette and labored up the steps, first having to perform the also degrading action of stating, "No, I don't need the ramp." I paid my fare and took my seat and folded my walker. And the fare I paid, half price. Oh yeah, baby, the benefits of being a cripple.

I arrived at nine Mulberry Street and made my way up to the third floor in the elevator. I had no idea what I would find there and as the elevator ascended, I tried to devise various strategies for possible scenarios. Unfortunately, I came up with nothing and knew I was going to have to go in blind and just deal with whatever the situation happened to be, on the spot and hope for the best. I just couldn't come up with anything during the elevator ride. Um, I did realize afterwards that the apartment was on the third floor so it was a very quick ride and there really was nowhere near enough time to conceivably have been able to do so. The elevator arrived at the third floor and I pushed open the door. As I did so, I contemplated the idea that maybe I should have deliberated on those questions during the period of time before arriving at the actual address. Oh well, live and learn. I hobbled on my walker to apartment thirty-two.

I reached the door and rang the bell. After a few moments, the door opened. Standing there was a woman. She greeted me with, "Yes, can I help you?" *Oh shit.* I realized at that moment I hadn't even bothered to figure out what I would say if someone actually answered the door. As I stood there trying to think up my response I realized I really, *really* hadn't thought this through very well. "I'm sorry but what is it you want?" the woman asked.

I tried to think up a good answer but saw nothing and decided I might as well just go with the truth and see where it would lead. "My apologies and I'm sure this will sound strange but I received instructions that I should come here."

The woman gave a puzzled look. "Instructions, what do you mean?"

I shook my head nervously. "I'm sorry. This all is rather odd to me, as well, but I received a telegram, of all things, if you can believe that, directing me so that I might find clues regarding a mystery I'm trying to solve."

"A telegram? Are you serious? I didn't think telegrams still existed. None of this is making any sense." she responded with apprehension.

"I know, and the instructions were written as a riddle which makes even less sense, but still, I followed them. Here, see for yourself. " I pulled out and handed the telegram to the woman.

She took it and read with a baffled look on her face. "Dear God. Who sent this?"

"I have no idea who the sender is." I answered.

"So, what is the mystery it is referring to, the one you were sent here to try and solve?" the woman asked.

I gestured with skepticism. "That's where things get even stranger. I first received another telegram that suggested the writer, Xavier Cockroachal Damon, who it is widely accepted is dead, isn't actually dead, after all and I have been tasked with finding him."

The woman got an astonished look on her face. "Wait a second, Xavier Cockroachal Damon, the absolute greatest writer of this or any generation, the most talented, renowned writer of all time. He may not actually be dead, you're saying?"

I shrugged. "Well, that's what the telegram said. I, myself have no idea."

The woman shook her head, perplexed. "But, but, that doesn't make sense. I mean, everyone knows Xavier Cockroachal Damon died at the end of The Case of the Ignonomous and Preposterous Hapeshalesh. I mean, that's common knowledge. Even my neighbor's dog knows that. Everyone does."

"I know, but, still, that's what the first telegram said. Here, let me show it to you." I pulled the other telegram from my pocket.

The woman shook her head. "No, come inside and I'll read it there. We have to get to the bottom of this. This is very intriguing. Please, come in."

We sat in the living room of her apartment. I was sipping from my bottle of vodka. She was sipping from a cup of tea. I had shown her the other telegram. I had learned her name was Olivia. She was actually quite attractive and seemed somewhat near my age, maybe a little younger.

Olivia had a curious look. "What I don't understand, what really confuses me here is, why would the person who sent this think there was any information I could provide that would help?"

"So there's nothing, nothing that could lead me to my next step?" I probed.

Olivia shook her head. "No. You saw how shocked I was when you told me. I know absolutely nothing about it."

"Hmm. Well, maybe the information that will lead to the next step is not direct knowledge but something in your life you are unaware of that does shed light on the situation." I hypothesized.

"Such as what?" she asked, perplexed.

I threw my hands up, flummoxed. "As for that, I have no idea. A person, a place, a phone number, whatever it may be, and maybe if we investigate that it will actually reveal some answers. Do you know of anything that might be of use in terms of that?"

"Not off the top of my head, that's for sure. I would have to go over all my records and see if anything stands out. I'm not sure it will do any good though because it really could be anything so I wouldn't even know what I would be looking for." she responded with uncertainty.

"You're right. This isn't going to be easy. It's going to be like finding a needle in a stack of needles." I commented with a grave tone.

She had a befuddled look. "Um. If it's just a big stack of needles, wouldn't it be quite easy to find a needle?"

"Well, yes, sure, a needle, but not the specific needle we're looking for. Finding that needle in a stack of needles will indeed be immeasurably more difficult than finding a needle in a haystack." I took a drink, realizing as I did so that my attempted witty twist on the old saying really did sound entirely idiotic and nonsensical.

"Well. All we can do is start. Just go over everything and maybe something will jump out at me." I then heard a key in the lock and the front door opening. Olivia looked down the hallway leading to the living room. She called out, "Oh, hi mom."

There then walked into the room an elderly woman wearing a long flowing gown and an ornate vest. It was the gypsy fortune teller who had come to my apartment. "Hello, my dearest, your mother is here." she announced. As she walked into the room she saw the two of us sitting there. She stopped, focusing on me with an icy stare. "What the hell are you doing here?" she turned to her daughter. "Olivia, what is this man doing here?"

"Oh, it's no problem, mother. He's just my visitor, it's perfectly fine." Olivia assured her.

The gypsy woman sneered at me. "No, it's not perfectly fine, he's an asshole! What the hell are you doing with my daughter?"

"Have the two of you met?" Olivia asked, surprised.

"Very briefly." I replied.

The gypsy woman pointed her finger at me, menacingly. "Get the hell out of here, do you hear me. Remember my prophecy. You will meet a goddess who will bring about your demise and doom, and I'll be damned if I'm going to allow you to be anywhere around my daughter when that happens, because I refuse for her to be any sort of collateral damage from your destruction!"

"Mother, don't you think you might be overreacting and being a bit overprotective?" Olivia remarked.

The mother shook her head confidently. "No. I saw the vision. I saw the future. This man will meet a goddess and she will bring about his end. I cannot knowingly allow you to have anything to do with this man. What kind of gypsy fortune teller would I be if I did?"

"I don't know, a really crappy one." I offered up.

The mother looked at me with venom. "Shut up, you stinking rat bastard!"

I responded with a diplomatic tone, "Well, I'm just saying, your whole reason for your animosity toward me is because you felt I was mocking you and my doing so would lead to me being cursed as punishment. To prove that you actually were a divine fortune teller, you offered up this prophecy that I would meet some Goddess and that, even though I would know it would bring about my downfall, still, I would dive head first into it."

The mother pointed at me knowingly. "Oh, indeed you will. Of that, I assure you. You never lie to a gypsy!"

"Really. Tell me, do you recall the reason you became so incensed, so enraged because you knew at that moment I was mocking your powers by lying to you? And, because you were certain I was mocking you, you prophesied that the mystical forces that govern us all would show me the error of my ways and I would encounter this, goddess, you say, that would bring about my downfall. And, all of this was destined to happen because you knew in that moment I was a liar?" I continued.

"Indeed, I do." the mother snarled.

"It's because I asked you to tell me the whereabouts of two individuals. Tell me, do you remember the names of those two individuals?" I asked.

"That I most certainly do." the mother responded with contempt.

"Olivia, would you be so kind as to tell your mother what it is we are attempting to do here?" I requested.

"We are trying to determine the whereabouts of Xavier Cockroachal Damon and Hurphuldurp Mahangahoo." Olivia answered.

The mother looked at her daughter with bewilderment. "What? Olivia, what the hell has gotten into you? Those obviously aren't the names of real people. What is wrong with you that you would fall for this stupidity and listen to this obvious mad man? Olivia, please, those aren't actual, real names."

Olivia looked at her mother with surprise. "But, mom, you really don't know? Xavier Cockroachal Damon is the absolute greatest writer of all time, possessing a skill of the written word that has never before been seen, nor will ever be seen again unless there is the second coming of a new literary God. As for Hurphuldurp Mahangahoo, well on that one, it is true that isn't a person's real name because it is now clear it was just Xavier Cockroachal Damon using the name and hiding his identity. But, it all comes back to Xavier Cockroachal Damon. It's all about Xavier Cockroachal Damon, the greatest writer in history. I thought everyone knew his name. Really, mother, I'm shocked you didn't."

"Jesus Christ, I really have to start reading something more that centuries old fortune telling tomes." the mother responded with embarrassment. She looked at me. "Well then, allow me to apologize to you for apparently being mistaken. That being so, and that my prophecy came about as a response to you mocking me, I now no longer believe it will come to be at all or that you are in any actual danger. Very well then, Olivia, I see no reason for you not to associate with this man. I'm sure no harm will befall you if you do. So then, I wish the both of you luck in your endeavours. Olivia, my dear, I am going to retire to my room to get some sleep."

"Good night, mother." Olivia replied.

"I'm sorry we got off on the wrong foot. Good night." I proclaimed.

"No problem. I see now it was a misunderstanding. Good night to you both and good luck on your quest." The mother turned and walked into her room and closed the door.

We talked for a little while more about what our next steps should be. We settled on Olivia checking all information she had that might shed light on why the sender of the telegram would send me to her, while I would examine other possible leads I could dig up that might reveal other avenues we could pursue and then we would talk again in a couple of days.

I did actually come up with one idea I thought could possibly be helpful but ultimately it was a dead end and led to more questions than answers. Since it was a telegram, I assumed there would have to be some sort of electronic trail accompanying it and if that could be traced then maybe it would reveal who the sender was. The telegram had written on it that it was transmitted by a company called "Telegram Express Delivery Incorporated". I decided I should look them up and bring the telegrams to one of their offices. The problem was, I could find absolutely no listings for an office for that company anywhere, nor even any information about "Telegram Express Delivery Incorporated", at all. I could find nothing whatsoever that showed the company even existed. It seemed it was just a phantom corporation. Beyond that, I couldn't even find anything that suggested telegrams were still in use, at all. I then wondered why I had so readily accepted that they were even real, actual, legitimate telegrams and not just correspondence that someone wanted to make look like a telegram? But, what possible reason could there be for someone to do that? What would be the point or purpose? I had absolutely no idea and was bewildered by it all, but what now seemed clear was that they were not real telegrams, because, as I originally suspected, it appeared telegrams no longer existed as a means of communication. The supposed telegrams were just messages that the person writing them wanted me to think were telegrams. Why would someone do that? None of it made any sense whatsoever and I was more confused than ever.

Over the next couple of days I came up with absolutely zero other possible leads that might reveal other avenues we could pursue. I mean, really now, where was I supposed to look? I had nothing to go on. Fortunately, I received a call from Olivia telling me she had found something that could be useful and we arranged to meet again at her apartment so she could relay the information.

We sat in the living room of Olivia's apartment. She spoke, "First, let me just say, if it's OK, it's nice to see you again. I actually really enjoyed meeting you."

"I enjoyed meeting you, too. I had no idea what to expect when I headed out to the address and I can say I was pleasantly surprised." I replied honestly.

"Oh, you're just saying that, I'm sure." she bashfully replied.

"No, really, I mean it. I'm actually going to enjoy working with you." I assured her.

"Well, anyway. I did find some things that were peculiar." she announced.

"Such as?" I asked.

"Well, in the past I have received emails and text messages from the same source. They would all just say, "Find The Answers to the Mystery You Seek to Solve". I thought nothing of it at the time and just disregarded them. There was no explanation, no further details, no clarification as to the nature of the sender, just that one line. I paid no attention to it, but looking at it now it seems very odd and I think it was someone talking about this." she explained.

I nodded my head, intrigued. "I have to admit, that is very odd. If it was some business or what have you, they would certainly elaborate more upon the nature of the business, not merely send some vague line like that. I think it's very likely that it's connected to the messages I received. But then?"

"What?" Olivia asked with a keen look.

I threw up my hands with exasperation. "Why are they sending you emails and text messages and are sending me freakin fake telegrams?"

"Maybe it's not actually the same person. Maybe it's different people sending messages about the same thing." she conjectured.

I took a drink from my bottle. "That's certainly possible. Sort of wish my guy could get a bit more technology literate but it's definitely worth looking into. Anything else?"

"Well, this one is more ominous. It was a letter I received some time ago and, at the time, I thought it was rather disturbing and held onto it in case I received others. I never did though, and so I just forgot about it until after we met." she revealed.

"What did the letter say?" I asked.

"I have it right here." she picked up the letter, "It says, 'I implore you to take care before embarking on a quest to find answers, for that journey is certain to be a perilous one. Sometimes, maybe answers are better left unresolved, for you may not like what you find. Proceed with caution and I think it might be for the better if you never proceeded at all. Your life may depend on it.'"

I was astonished at what she had read. "Holy shit, I see why you would be a bit alarmed. Was there a return address?"

She shook her head. "None."

"Was there anything else in the letter?" I asked.

She shook her head. "Nothing. Only what I read to you."

"I see. Yes, that is certainly bizarre." I scratched my head in thought, "And it arrived in the normal mail?"

Olivia nodded her head. "Yes."

"I see." I nodded, as well with a curious look, "Normal postal mail and I get fake telegrams."

"What do you think it all means?" she asked.

I paused for a moment to collect my thoughts. "You know, I think we have to consider the possibility that this is all just someone playing a practical joke on us. I mean, I told you the supposed telegrams are always delivered by someone dressed as a bellhop who keeps insisting I'm a guest at the hotel he works for, which is in no way true. That might be a hint. Then, for you to receive that disturbing letter and the other messages."

"But, why would they send them to you and me, for what purpose?" Olivia asked, perplexed.

I shrugged. "Maybe they just wanted us to meet. Maybe it's someone trying to set us up together. Maybe it's some matchmaker, dating site run out of an insane asylum, who knows."

She dismissed the joke. "Oh, that's ridiculous. There's no way a guy like you would go for a girl like me."

I looked at her, puzzled. "Why would you say that? Of course I would."

"You're just saying that." she commented timidly.

"No, really, I mean it." I emphasized my words so she would know I was being sincere. "If it's a dating site run out of an insane asylum, I'd say the lunatics running the asylum actually know what they're doing."

She appeared embarrassed. "You're just saying that so my feelings don't get hurt."

"I'm really not. I mean it." I pronounced with exasperation. "So, would you, you know, want to go out on an actual romantic date?"

She blushed and nodded her head with satisfaction. "Yes. Yes, I would."

I nodded my head as well. "OK then, cool."

"But, I do think we need to look into these things and see if they might be true. It may very well be genuine and actually is someone trying to tell us Xavier Cockroachal Damon is still alive." she theorized.

"Absolutely. It may all just be a practical joke but it may actually not be. We have to get to the bottom of this, whatever this may be. We have to find out the truth." I concurred.

Over the next few days, we examined the leads as to where the emails and messages were coming from but it led nowhere. Literally, it led to nowhere. The domain that had sent them no longer existed. It was gone, so trying to follow them to a source was a dead end. It certainly was strange that the only communications that were traceable had been scrubbed from existence, leaving only fake telegrams and a letter that had no address that could be investigated. Why would someone do that? The idea that this was all just a big hoax was certainly seeming a more credible explanation.

During this time, me and Olivia actually had our actual date and, well, it went very well. We both had a really good time. I made her laugh. She, well, never actually made me laugh, but that's just because I never actually laugh, but I really did like being with her and she, for some inexplicable reason, seemed to actually really like being with me. At the end of the night, I actually kissed her, hoping there would in fact be other nights like it.

And there were. In the weeks that followed, many times we would get together to do whatever, watch a movie, watch a, not going to even attempt to deny it, *really* crappy TV show she wanted to watch which I never would have watched on my own but didn't mind at all watching with her, or go out and sit on a bench or just talk, go to a restaurant, whatever the case may be, but really all of it was only ever to be together and be with each other. During this time our physical interactions also progressed considerably. I'm not giving any details, I'm not that kind of guy, but you can probably figure it out. And it was all, dare I say, actually all very enjoyable which is strange because I never actually enjoyed anything. We got along really great, and in the end, whatever we did, I just genuinely liked being around her, which is strange because I never actually liked being around anybody. It was all very, very strange but strange in a good way, which itself was strange because that was a type of strange I had never actually known before.

I was sitting in my apartment, drinking from a glass of vodka. Olivia was coming over later and I was looking forward to that. It wasn't to examine other leads in terms of the investigation we were on as we had nothing to go on. It was just to be together and that was fine with me. I finished my glass and pulled out and lit a cigarette. The doorbell rang. She wasn't supposed to come over for several hours. 'Maybe she was early.' I thought to myself. If so, that would be a nice surprise. I walked with my cane over to the door and opened it. Standing outside was the man dressed as a bellhop who always insisted this was a hotel.

I reacted with annoyance. "Oh, God, what do you want?"

"It is not what I want that is important, what matters is what you want and how I might provide it for you. That is my job, working here at the hotel. So tell me, fine sir, is there anything you want?" the man graciously replied.

"Yes, for you to get it through your damn head that this isn't a damn hotel. Really, who the hell are you?" I growled at him, having run out of any patience for these episodes long ago.

"Why, I am but an employee, sent up from the front desk to make sure all of our guests are having a satisfactory stay at our establishment." replied the man.

"No, stop it, really." I snapped at him. "There is no front desk and this is not your establishment. What did you, escape from a psych ward? I don't know what the hell is going on here but I want you to leave now, and if you are so insistent that this is a hotel, put a permanent do not disturb sign on the door and never bother me again."

The man nodded his head amicably. "Very well then, if that is what you wish, but, first, I should inform you that I have something for you from the front desk."

I groaned. "Let me guess, another telegram."

The man smiled widely. "Indeed. Here you are, sir." The man handed me a large envelope.

"Hmm, you know, I find it funny that there is never any indication of who the sender is. Now, I look at how you are dressed and it is rather archaic. Tell me, it wouldn't by any chance be you who is typing up these supposed telegrams, now would it? A telegram itself is an archaic form of communication only used long ago, wouldn't you agree? Would be rather fitting, now wouldn't it?" I theorized.

The man gave a perplexed look. "I assure you, sir, I am unaware what you are referring to. I myself would never violate your privacy by looking at the actual content of the telegram that was sent to you. It is merely my job to deliver them to you. My apologies, sir if you are disappointed with my job performance."

"I didn't say you were reading them, I am asking are you writing them?" I accused him.

The man shook his head with a befuddled look. "You have me confused, sir. Writing telegrams is not one of my job responsibilities. I do not know what you mean."

"Yes, well I assure you that you have me more confused. All that I want is a clear answer. Who are you? And what is going on here?" I was trying to get to the bottom of what was going on.

The man smiled cheerfully. "Who I am is an employee here to ensure your stay at our hotel is a pleasant experience and to provide you with whatever you may need to make that the case."

"Failing miserably." I deadpanned.

"Again, sir, I apologize if my job performance is not up to your standards. If you have any complaints you are free to voice them with the front desk. Regardless, I will do my best to better serve your needs." the man expounded, contrite. "I will leave you to your business. Do not hesitate to call down to the front desk if there is anything else I can do for you. Farewell, sir, I hope you enjoy your day." The man turned and walked away and I closed the door.

Seriously, what the hell was going on here? The person seemed absolutely convinced he was working in a hotel. He betrayed no sign at all of that categorically being untrue. Maybe he was just a really good actor commissioned to play the role. But, by whom? And why? Why on earth would anybody send me on a quest to find out if Xavier Cockroachal Damon was still alive? I mean, really, why would anybody actually do that? It really did seem the only explanation was that all of this was just a grand practical joke being perpetrated by someone. But, why? The only thing I knew for sure was that none of this made any sense, at all. I shook my head then walked with my cane and sat on the bed. I poured myself a drink.

I opened the telegram and read it. It said, "I warn you, these are perilous times. One misstep could prove disastrous. You must work harder and figure out how to actually find Xavier Cockroachal Damon, That is, if he is, in fact still alive, which is something you must first determine. You must work quickly for time is of the essence. If Xavier Cockroachal Damon does still live and, when swept over the waterfall, did not actually meet his watery grave, I fear his end will actually soon come to be. Find Xavier Cockroachal Damon and you will find your answers. You must hurry though, for his life depends on it. And, so does your own, for you have started down a path of great danger and if you are not careful it may well lead to your demise, as well. I wish I could say more but I'm sorry, I cannot. What I can do is give you another clue to assist you on your quest. You should journey to Randall's Island Park. Once there, you must walk amongst the walkway that traverses Hell's Gate. Look for a weathered bench that sits near the edge of the water. It is right next to a large oak tree. Inside the opening of the tree, you will find a key. Sit on the bench and look for a craggy crevice in the wood. Inside the craggy crevice you will find a small box. The key will open the box. I wish you the best of luck in your endeavours. There are forces at work you cannot, as of yet, possibly understand. I hope you are successful. I'm sorry, but that is all I am able to say at the moment. I wish I could say more."

Are you motherfuckin kidding me? You wish you could say more? Um, apparently you really, *really* can. In fact it seems you know exactly where Xavier Cockroachal Damon is. So why don't you just come out and tell me? And I'm supposed to go find a bench and a tree and find a key then fumble around in a craggy crevice to find a box the key will open. How needlessly convoluted is that? And I don't want to go fumbling around in some bench's craggy crevice. I think the bench's craggy crevice should be left alone and remain unmolested. Is there not a more direct, less ridiculous manner in which the clue could be presented? And what of these cryptic comments about Xavier Cockroachal Damon's life, as well as my own depending on it? Care to elaborate would you, maybe? And the instructions were to walk along the walkway that traverses Hell's Gate. Sure, that in no way sounds ominous. The only thing about the message that made any sense was the line about dealing with forces I couldn't possibly understand. You got me, no argument there. I shook my head with bewilderment and drank from my glass.

I sat and tried to figure out what was going on here. As I did, I came up with a possible explanation. After receiving the first telegram, I considered the possibility that it was actually Xavier Cockroachal Damon, himself who had sent it but immediately dismissed that theory because it didn't make any sense. Now, as I sat there I began to consider that that might actually be the case. I don't know, maybe Xavier Cockroachal Damon had actually decided to make his return and this was a publicity stunt to signal his return or something.

Now, on the surface that would really seem to be stupid and make no sense and how would that possibly accomplish anything? But, to this, one really must take into consideration that, during his life, Xavier Cockroachal Damon's actions quite often made no discernible sense whatsoever and that, much of the time, he really was a complete drunken idiot, so, in actuality it would be very much like him. Yes, the more I thought about it, the more sense it made. It was absurd, nonsensical, void of any beneficial purpose, reckless, and incredibly complicated for no functional purpose and, in the end, incredibly, incredibly stupid. It was very much an Xavier Cockroachal Damon thing to do. Olivia would be here in a couple hours. When she got here, I would show her the message and let her know what my new theory was as to what was going on.

Olivia and I sat on the bed, she having just read the telegram. "Wow, that's really something. So, what do you make of it?"

I thought deeply, examining all the possibilities. "Well, I've been thinking about it and I now think it's actually Xavier Cockroachal Damon, himself who is sending these."

"Really? So you don't actually think it's someone else who is sending them?" Olivia questioned.

I sighed with exasperation. "That's what I'm going with right now."

"Hmm. Well, I really think you should consider the explanation that it is actually someone else who just really wants you to find Xavier Cockroachal Damon." Olivia hypothesized.

I threw up my hands in consternation. "But then, why like this? Why in this way? It doesn't actually make any sense."

"Well, I suppose there would be no way to know for sure what their reasons are unless you were actually able to find Xavier Cockroachal Damon. If you do that then all the answers will be clear. I think it would be a mistake to outright conclude it's just Xavier Cockroachal Damon, himself sending these to you." Olivia surmised.

I exhaled, frustrated. "Well, I haven't outright concluded anything. I'm just trying to come up with something that makes sense. It's what I'm going with right now because none of this makes any sense. The most obvious explanation would be that it's just the guy who keeps delivering them who is writing them, but, I don't know, I honestly don't think that's the case. I truly do believe he has no idea what is written on them." I shook my head, "Do you have any ideas?"

"Well, the person who keeps delivering them to you, the person who keeps insisting this is a hotel, I think there must be something there. Why does he keep doing that?" Olivia wondered.

I shook my head and took a drink. "I have no idea."

"Is there some reason a hotel would be significant to you?" Olivia probed.

"No." I simply answered, flummoxed.

"No reason at all?" Olivia pressed.

I took another drink from my glass. "Nothing."

"Are you sure?" Olivia asked, pointedly.

I threw my hands up in the air. "Yes."

Olivia took on a pensive look. "There must be something though, there has to be some meaning for it? You can't think of anything? Think hard."

"No. I see nothing." I pronounced, exasperated. "Look, I really just think he's some actor, either hired by Xavier Cockroachal Damon, himself or someone else."

Olivia nodded her head with a quizzical look on her face. "Still, there must be some reason whoever is sending it would choose to recreate a hotel setting. You should really give it some thought and see if something comes to you. If you could answer that question, I think it would be very good. It has to be relevant."

I shrugged and drank again from my glass. "Well, I'll try but I can't think of what it could be."

Olivia nodded her head with certainty. "You should. I think it's important."

"I will, but what else do you think we should do?" I asked.

"Well, I think we have to go check out the park. See if the things the message said are actually there." she suggested.

"As I said before, I think this may all just be someone playing a joke." I responded with doubt.

"That may actually be the case but we have to find out for sure. Maybe we go to the park and the objects aren't actually there, then we'll know. Or maybe they will actually be there and we find out what's in the box and what it tells us. We have to keep following the leads until we know for sure." Olivia announced with determination.

"No, you're right, we do. I know nothing for sure yet so we have to keep exploring all options." I conceded.

"So, how do we get to Randall's Island?" Olivia inquired.

"I have absolutely no clue. It's an island off of, or technically part of Manhattan. I wanted to show you the message first before I found out. Now that we're going to go, I'll look it up." I replied.

"And what of this walking over Hell's Gate. That sounds a bit disconcerting." Olivia asked with some trepidation.

I took a drink from my glass. "That one I already did look up before you got here because it was admittedly, a bit unsettling. You see, one of the sides of Randall's Island, the part between it and Queens, is separated by the East River. Hell's Gate is a small part of it that historically is known for being extremely turbulent with very dangerous water currents, thus the reason for the name."

"I see. So then, the plan is, we find out how to get to Randall's Island, go to the park and walk along the portion that Hell's Gate flows along and find the bench. We can do that." Olivia buoyantly exclaimed.

"We can do that and we can completely waste our time doing that." I countered with skepticism.

"But, who knows, I mean, right now you are doubting whether this is just some wild goose chase and none of it is real but maybe the answers are to be found at the water's edge and maybe at the end, you actually will find Xavier Cockroachal Damon. Wouldn't you like that?" Olivia asked.

"Yes, actually I would." I admitted.

"So would I." Olivia chimed with enthusiasm.

I sat in the living room of Olivia's apartment. The plan was to meet there then head over to the park. She greeted me at the door but said she needed a little more time to get ready. I waited there, sitting on the couch. As I sat there, the front door opened. Into the room, walked her mother, the gypsy fortune teller.

"Hello." I greeted her.

She got a queasy look when she saw me. "Oh, it's *you*."

"Yes, how are you?" I asked.

She sighed heavily. "Oh, busy day, busy day, very tired. Rough day, very rough day."

"I'm sorry to hear that." I attempted to console her.

She looked at me with a serious, mournful look. "Yes, yes, but do you want to know the worst part of my day?"

"What?" I asked.

Her expression became very angry. "Seeing you! I do not like you. You make me sick. I don't know what the hell my daughter is thinking or what the hell is wrong with her and what the hell has gotten into her." Probably don't need to point this out, but she spoke with a tone of disdain.

"I'm sorry to hear that, as well." I bashfully exclaimed.

The expression on her face became totally mystified. "Look, I don't know what sort of demon, mind manipulation powers you are drawing from but there is no way my daughter would have anything to do with the likes of you. You are no good. Her associating with you will only bring her heartache and pain. You are a dark stain on the beautiful light of her soul. Being around you will only bring her chaos, tragedy and catastrophe. You are a dark curse that will infect all that are foolish enough to be around you. I don't know how she can't see it. How can she be so blind? You will only ever lead to the damnation and downfall of anyone who doesn't wake up to the fact that you are a dark force, miserable, useless, pestilent sludge, grotesque, rotten ghoul!"

"Eh." I, um, eh'd. Really, what else is there to say?

She pointed her finger at me, threateningly. "You listen to me. I will do everything in my power to get my daughter to see the error of her ways before it is too late. I will rescue her and save her from your evil clutches before you do any serious damage. If I must, I will stab a sacred dagger into that worthless, already dead heart of yours so that my dear daughter will never have to suffer any consequences from knowing you, you miserable, worthless, demon turd!"

Olivia walked into the room. "OK, I'm ready to go. Oh, mother, you're home. You two talking about anything interesting?"

"Oh, I was merely reminding him to always treat my dearest daughter as she deserves." She gave me the, I'm watching you hand gesture, with a severe, cutting stare.

I nodded my head uncomfortably, picked up my backpack from the floor and put it on then stood. "Yeah. that's all. It was a good chat, but we should get going."

Olivia and I walked through Randall's Island Park, looking for the bench, me hobbling along on my walker. "Well, at least it's a nice day." I commented.

"A very nice day." Olivia announced with a smile.

"I always think it's best that the weather is pleasant when I go sticking my hand in a tree's hole and probe a bench's craggy crevice." I observed whimsically.

Olivia scowled at me. "Don't be dirty. I'm going to start getting jealous."

"You do realize we might not actually find anything." I pointed out.

"I know that, but we have to see." Olivia urged.

I shrugged dismissively. "I know, but I still have a feeling we'll just be chasing our own tails in some meaningless diversion."

"Say that's the case, it was still a nice day to go for a walk and sit on a bench in the park." Olivia remarked.

"Always the glass half full kind of person, aren't you." I observed.

"And you, always the glass half empty kind of person." Olivia pointed out.

I shook my head. "No. I'd say I'm more of a, who the hell has been drinking out of my glass, kind of person."

Olivia stopped and pointed to a tree. I stopped, as well. "Wait, see that tree over there next to that bench. I think that's what we're looking for."

I looked at where she was pointing. "I don't see any other benches directly next to trees anywhere else, so you may very well be right. Let's go check."

We walked over to the tree by the bench. There was that circular hole common to oak trees. I reached my hand inside and felt around. I felt something and pulled it out. It was a key.

"So, there is a key." Olivia commented.

I shrugged. "Yeah, let's check out the bench and see what we find."

We went and sat down on the bench. Sure enough, there was a portion of it that was worn away in a craggy pattern.

"That must be it. See what's in there." Olivia directed me.

I felt around inside the worn away part of the bench but wasn't finding anything. "OK, so I'm fingering around inside the bench's craggy crevice."

Olivia spoke, a tone of anger within her playful remark. "You seem to be enjoying it. I think I'm going to have to kill this bitch, whore bench with a chainsaw."

"I promise you, the bench means nothing to me." I reassured her.

"Oh, and that's supposed to make it better? Oh sure, I fucked her but don't worry, she means nothing to me." Olivia scoffed with jealousy.

"I have no intention of fucking the bench." I stated, still searching for the object we were supposed to find.

"Why don't you just hurry up and find whatever's in there or I will never speak to you again. I'll just let you run off to live with your slut bench." Olivia threatened.

"I think someone may be getting a wee bit testy here. But, the problem is I'm not finding anything, I don't think there's anything here, I mean," my hand connected with something, "wait a second. I think I may have something. I think it's tape. Hold on." I peeled off the tape and dislodged what I had found. It was a small, metal box. "Voila." I held the box up to show Olivia.

Olivia sneered at me. "Was it good for you, too?"

"I assure you, I took no pleasure in it, it was only business." I methodically stated.

Olivia smirked at me. "Whore. Is there a keyhole?"

"There is." I announced.

"Use the key and see what's inside. I'm very curious." Olivia enthusiastically urged me.

I looked at the box I held in my hand. "It's really quite small. There can't be much but let's find out." I used the key and turned the lock of the box. I pulled open the lid. Inside the box there was another key and a small piece of paper. The box was also filled with rose petals. "A key, a small piece of paper and some rose petals."

"What's on the paper?" Olivia asked.

"Let's see." I took the small piece of paper out of the box and set the box on the bench. I looked at the paper. "It says in big letters, CubeSmart Self Storage and there is an address beneath it. It also has written on it, unit 248."

"So that's what the key is for, unit 248." Olivia surmised.

"There is also written on it, the words, Electronic Gate Code, followed by numbers. That I imagine is to get access to the facility." I assumed.

"I wonder what's inside the storage unit?" Olivia wondered.

I was feeling very dubious about it all. "Yes, well I wonder why somebody would provide us with full, unfettered access to their storage unit."

"Those things can be pretty big, can't they?" Olivia mentioned.

"Exactly. So why would someone provide us with free access to the facility and the unit where we can come and go as we please, and take everything in the storage unit if we so desired. Unless the storage unit is being rented solely for the purpose of what we are supposed to find in it." I shook my head, "It doesn't make any sense."

"I guess that is what it's for. I mean, whoever it is that gave us the key wouldn't leave their own personal belongings in it, too, hoping we weren't in a pilfering mood that day. The whole point of the unit must just be for the clues we will find." Olivia postulated.

"Yeah, but why would someone do that?" I had a very puzzled look, "It doesn't make any sense."

"But, what is in the storage unit? I mean, it could be anything. This is so exciting. I wonder what we'll find." Olivia radiated with excitement and adventure.

I shook my head. "Um, probably just another key. Look, problem here. We're sent to go investigate a tree where we will find a key that will open a box. When we open the box we merely find another key. So then, why not just put the little box inside the tree? It would have been a much better place for it then some craggy crevice of some rotted bench. So, why not just do that?"

"Well, we wouldn't have been able to open the little box if we hadn't found the first key." Olivia observed.

"Um, well, I think you're missing my point. There's no reason the little box had to itself be locked. Why find a key to just find another key? What, is this just someone with a surplus of keys they are trying to find some use for?" I explained.

"Maybe it's a metaphor. Keys represent unlocking the truth, getting to the true answer, actually finding Xavier Cockroachal Damon. Open the locks and all truth will be revealed." Olivia theorized.

I shook my head, unconvinced. "Yes, well this in no way dispels the theory that this is all just some grand practical joke being played on us. And why the hell was the little box filled with rose petals?"

Olivia got a queer, inquisitive look of purpose. "I imagine rose petals have a special significance to the person leaving the clues. I know you are skeptical and think all of this is just a hoax but I just have this feeling, I feel it in my gut, that if we keep following the clues you'll see, you will actually find Xavier Cockroachal Damon. I just really have this feeling and I think keys and rose petals will somehow be shown to be important for some reason. I mean, why would they have bothered to put the rose petals in the box if it didn't have some meaning? Come on, we have to keep following the leads, we can't stop now."

"I'm not saying to just stop now. I mean, we have the key for the storage unit so there's no excuse to not go see what's inside it. I just have a feeling there won't be anything of value or of any use, that it's all just a big joke. But, certainly, we have the key so we have to go see." I concluded.

"Who knows, maybe there actually will be something important." Olivia intensely beamed with inspiration.

Olivia and I met the next morning and headed over to the CubeSmart location written on the note. We put in the numbers listed as the gate keycode into the outer door of the facility. Sure enough, it opened and we were inside the facility and walking toward unit 248. She was overwhelmed with enthusiasm at what we would find, me, less so. We walked through the facility, me hobbling along on my walker, wearing my backpack.

"You keep saying there won't be anything there but how do you know?" Olivia questioned.

"Call it a hunch." I answered flatly.

"Well, I still think we'll find something really important." she eagerly beamed.

"I have to say, I admire your optimism." I responded with sarcasm.

"You do have to say that because if you didn't, I'd never speak to you again." she snidely replied.

"And that's why I said it. I didn't actually mean it but I said it, all the same." I conceded.

She blew me a kiss. "Oh, so sweet."

I stopped and she did as well, me looking at a storage unit. "Here it is, unit 248." It was a small unit, probably about four feet by six feet.

"That it's a small locker type unit rather than one of those giant room sized units makes sense if it's only here for the clues we will find. Open it up, let's see what's inside." she eagerly announced.

"Let's find out." I stated, eagerness in no way making an appearance.

"It could be anything. This is so exciting." she, well, excitedly commented.

I took out the key and unlocked the storage unit, pulling the door open. Inside, on a shelf, there was another key and a note and the locker throughout was filled with rose petals. "Wow. Another key. And the damn thing is filled with rose petals. And there's a note."

"What does the note say?" she enthusiastically asked.

I picked up the note and read it. "It says, 'Finding a Cockroachal can be difficult when he is hiding as someone else, but do not abandon your quest for you are getting close.'"

Olivia's face scrunched with confusion. "That's it?"

"That's it." I said.

"What's the key for?" she asked.

I looked closely at the key. "I don't know. There's a number on it, 37, but no other identifying information."

"And the note doesn't say?" she queried.

"No. I read the entire note to you." I explained.

Olivia had a puzzled look. "Is it for another storage unit?"

"I don't know what it's for." I replied.

"It has the number 37 on it. I think we should go to unit 37 and see if the key works on that lock." Olivia suggested.

"Um, so we are given a key and directed to a storage unit that inside only has another key for another storage unit. What kind of madness would that be?" I remarked on the absurdity of it all.

"But we have to at least go try." Olivia implored me.

"Of course we do." I agreed. "I mean, all we have is a key with the number 37 on it. We have nothing else to go on. We have to go and see if it opens that unit. If it does though, I'm going to need to get really drunk."

We walked back to storage unit 37. It was a much larger unit. Olivia looked at the door with interest. "Oh my, this one is much bigger. I wonder what could be in there."

I exhaled tiredly and exaggerated my words plaintively and mockingly, "Maybe the point of this is some new game show called

Collect The Keys and we'll open it up and there will be a guy who shouts, 'You just won. A new car.' as he points to a car next to him. Then we can get in the car and drive away, you driving of course because I'm going to be getting drunk and we can drive as far away from this craziness and never look back."

Olivia looked at me and smirked. "I think it's past your bedtime and you're getting cranky. Why not just try the lock and see, and then we can go back home."

"Sure, let's find out what awaits us." I took the key we had found in the other storage locker and tried it in the lock on storage unit 37. It wouldn't budge. It didn't turn at all. "Nothing. No good. It's not the key for this lock."

"Are you sure? Try harder." Olivia suggested.

"I'm telling you, it's not the key for this lock. Trying harder won't do any good." I handed the key to Olivia. "Here, try for yourself."

Olivia took the key and tried it in the lock. "You're right. This isn't the key for this lock." She looked at me, stymied, "So, what do we do?"

"Well, I say the first thing we do is get out of the facility. There are cameras here, you know. It is monitored, and if we don't get out of here, there's going to be a call to the police about two people trying to break into storage unit 37. Come on, let's go out to the sidewalk. I can at least have a cigarette that way." I proposed as our immediate course of action.

"OK" Olivia simply replied.

We exited the storage facility and stood at the corner of the street on the sidewalk. I was leaning my forearms on my walker, smoking a cigarette.

"So there wasn't anything else in the locker, maybe something we missed when we first looked.? Maybe we should go back and check again to make sure." Olivia inquired.

I stood fully and threw up my hands. I just realized I'm actually doing that quite a bit as events play out, but I threw up my hands in exasperation. "We already checked. There was nothing. Just all those damn rose petals."

"So, how do we figure out what the key is used for if it didn't open another storage unit?" she wondered.

I took a drag from my cigarette and sighed with resignation. "It's used for nothing. Come on, we're sent to go find a key to open a box that only has another key and when we use that key all we get is another key. This is ridiculous. Forget a wild goose chase, this is just a wild key chase and I'm sick of it."

"So, what do we do?" Olivia asked, earnestly.

I realized the futility of the question. "What can we do? We now have another key only we have no idea what this other key is for. What are we supposed to do, just go around the city trying it on every random lock we come across, hoping at some point it opens something?"

"But it has to be for something. We just have to figure it out." she speculated with consternation.

I took another drag from my cigarette then flicked it away to the sidewalk. I gently placed my hand on her shoulder and looked into her eyes. "Look, you have to just accept that this is someone playing a prank on us. And what's with all the damn rose petals? I mean, is someone trying to tell us Xavier Cockroachal Damon is alive and opened a flower shop?"

"There has to be some significance for it." she fervidly asserted.

I placed my hand gently on her cheek. "There's no significance to any of this. I know you want to believe, but this is ridiculous. It's like that, that, Russian doll thing or whatever it is, where every time you open one of the damn dolls there's just another damn doll, or something like that, if that's even what it is. I'm not sure I'm remembering correctly here which may very well entirely derail my intended point, though I assure you, the point I was trying to make is solid. Christ, what is that thing called?"

"Babushka Dolls." she responded.

I emphatically held my finger up. "Exactly, Babushka Dolls. I couldn't have said it better, myself."

"They are at times also just referred to as Russian Dolls so there really wasn't need for further clarification." Olivia explained.

I more emphatically held up my finger. "And that's exactly my point. I mean, the person leaving the clues says we are getting close, but, we haven't actually done anything. We haven't figured anything out. All we've done is follow the steps we were told to do, meaning, whoever this person is already knows all the answers. It's just going to end with us being told to go to some location where I bet, Xavier Cockroachal Damon will be waiting for us and he'll say, 'So you've found me. Well done.' Well, we'd only be finding him because he told us exactly where to go to find him because he's just toying with us."

"So, you really think it's actually Xavier Cockroachal Damon doing all this?" she asked with uncertainty.

I shrugged, doing a lot of that too I'm now realizing. "I don't know. There's a very good chance but there's no way to know for sure. Maybe it is someone else but what I do know is that whoever it is, is just toying with us. We weren't enlisted to solve some great mystery because whoever it is already knows everything, knows all the answers. It would just be as simple as them telling us, rather than leaving us like a couple of rats in a maze, chasing their own tails, looking for a piece of cheese. And you know what? I'm sick of it. I'm tired of this. I'm tired of being played for a fool. I'm tired of this damn game and I've had enough."

"So then you're giving up?" Olivia lamented with obvious disappointment in her voice.

I softly caressed her cheek. "Look, like I said, we're not even doing anything here. We're just being told things when whoever this is decides to tell us. I imagine they'll just reveal everything when they see fit to do so. Until then, I'm not even going to worry or even think about it."

"But, what about the key?" she asked with frustration.

"What of it? We have a key that we have absolutely no idea what it's used for. We could go back over everything and look for clues where maybe they did tell us without stating it outright, only, I already know there's nothing there. It's a dead end. There's nothing we can do with the key." I rationalized.

"It's a shame, though. I actually really liked going on this quest with you." she proclaimed, upset.

"And I really liked going on it with you. And please know, I don't at all think this has all been a waste. It led me to you and I really like being with you, which is crazy because I never like being around anybody. But, I really do like being with you and I'm actually very grateful this quest gave me that. But, I like being with you. I don't need this quest anymore and I don't even care anymore. I just want to be with you." I responded, not a word that was untrue.

Olivia smiled happily. "I'm glad to hear you say that. Here I was thinking as soon as the quest was done, you'd just be done with me, discarded like yesterday's paper, because you wanted something better to look at and be with."

I shook my head and talked with honest emotion. "Why can't you ever just accept I really do want to be with you? To hell with the damn quest. Come on, this gringy, grimy sidewalk is getting old. Let's get out of here, on to greener pastures together."

Olivia just stared into my eyes for a moment then asked, "Is that really what your heart wants?"

"My heart belongs to you." I pronounced, unable to think I would have ever spoken those words in truth to anyone, but knowing that I, indeed just had done so.

Olivia smiled with even more emotion. "Oh my, I feel so flattered. I always figured your heart would always belong to another."

I gave her a light kiss. "Come on, let's go. I'd say take my hand, only, then I wouldn't be able to walk, but the sentiment is there."

Olivia giggled. "Oh, come now, you say that only because you don't actually want to offer your hand to me, for if you did, I would indeed accept it. But, yes, let's leave, there are many better places we could be together. Hopefully someday we'll find the best place of them all."

I sat in the living room of Olivia's apartment while she was getting ready. We were heading out, not to pursue any leads of finding Xavier Cockroachal Damon, we had none to go on, and to be honest, I preferred that. The quest was old and tired and I was glad to be done with it. I, indeed did enjoy our time pursuing leads but only because I was with her and, in truth, I always preferred the times we were together just to be together. Tonight we were going out to dinner and going to an art gallery. Going to an art gallery was something she always wanted to do but had never actually done before, so I said, "Why don't we just go?" and tonight we were.

I sat on the couch and the front door opened. Into the room, walked Olivia's gypsy mother.

"Hello." I greeted her.

"Oh, it's you. Hello there." She spoke as she looked at me, but without the hateful venom usually accompanying the words when she did. OK, something was very wrong here, invasion of the body snatchers, anyone?

I saw an opening and an inroad for peace between us and I wanted to take advantage of the moment. "Look, I know you don't like me much but I really do like Olivia and, just know, I will always do my best to do right by her and be the best I can be for her, I promise."

She sighed. "You know. I can be a bit overprotective of my daughter. I admit that. It can cloud my judgment. But, maybe I was wrong about you. Maybe you're not so completely, terribly bad."

"Um, thank you?" I stammered, realizing this was by far the best she had ever spoken of me.

She spoke with an actually sincere, apologetic voice, "Look, my daughter's been hurt before and I just want to make sure that never happens again. I have no idea who he was. I knew nothing of him. She had never even mentioned him until after it ended, but she was very broken up about it. So now, if I know she's involved with someone, I keep a very watchful eye to make sure they stay in line and it doesn't happen again."

I tried to reassure her but in a genuine way, "Look, I can't promise anything because no one can promise that and anyone who does is just telling you what you want to hear and it's meaningless. But, I absolutely do promise you, I will do everything I can to make sure that never happens."

She looked at me thoughtfully. "Hmm, an honest and honorable answer, I like that. Well, there is something I can promise you, as well. I promise you that if that ever did happen again, I would crush that scoundrel fiend like the little bug he is and torch his corpse as a bonfire to his depravity."

I nodded my head. "No pressure or anything."

She nodded her head as well, giving a stern look. "No, no pressure. A promise. But, believe it or not, I actually sort of like you. I do believe you will do right by my daughter and won't let her down. Therefore, as for your relationship, you have my blessing."

"Thank you, that means a lot." I replied, honestly grateful and entirely surprised.

"Just, always treat her well." she advised.

I nodded my head sincerely. "I will."

Olivia came walking into the room from her bedroom. "Oh, hi mother. How did work go, any takers?"

Her mother sat down on a plush chair in the living room and sighed with exhaustion. "No. None. Actually, now that I think of it, there really never actually are. I actually have absolutely no idea why I keep doing this. Suppose I should consult the oracle to ask why am I so bloody stupid. I think I'm just going to set up a table in the park so at least I can sit and not have to walk around all the time."

Olivia responded with encouragement, "I think that's a very good idea. That way you wouldn't have to be on your feet all day." She picked up her purse from the couch and I picked up and put on my backpack and stood up, gripping my walker. "Well, me and Aaron are going out to the art gallery and then dinner so we really should be going."

Her mother nodded her head. "Yes, you run along now and I hope you have a wonderful evening."

Olivia smiled excitedly. "Oh, we will, bye mother."

"Goodbye darling." her mother said to Olivia.

Grateful for the startling turn in our dealings I sincerely stated, "Have a good night. It was a pleasure talking to you."

She replied, in a seemingly sincere way. "Yes, you have a good night, as well. Please enjoy your time with my daughter. Goodbye."

I sat in my apartment, drinking from a glass of vodka and smoking a cigarette.

The doorbell rang. I got up and walked over with my cane, taking a drag from the cigarette that I held with my other hand. It was the same man, dressed as a bellhop as he was the other times. He spoke, "Greetings, sir. And how might you be enjoying our hotel this day?"

I took a drag from my cigarette and I shook my head dismissively with agitation. "Not even going to bother. Not even going to waste my time. I believe you have a telegram for me."

The man flashed a beaming smile. "Why, that I do, sir, however did you know? Did you call down to the front desk and they told you?"

"Yeah, that's exactly what happened, so give me the telegram." I smugly, sarcastically answered.

The man pulled out a large envelope and handed it to me. "Here you are, sir. And remember, if there is anything—" I slammed the door shut and walked over to my bed with the fake telegram and sat down.

I felt actual dismay. I had actually been quite pleased to be done with all this and just spend time with Olivia, but here it was, another damn, fake telegram. Well, nothing else to do but open it up and see what it said. I tore it open and read. It said, "If you have two and then add three, what is it then that you see? But, to get to your destination, what is the avenue you should take to get there? Ah yes, a question. I think you might want to try an Avenue where you can Park. And, you know, I hear Amsterdam is nice this time of year, a wonderful time to wander a street, maybe you should go check it out. Maybe you can even find the type of place people stay when travelling. But how to find that place when you are on, excuse me, in Amsterdam. I don't know, maybe you should look back to the first question of the riddle. But, once there, if you are able to find it, oh me, oh my, so many rooms, so many, many rooms, but what could possibly be the room you seek. Hmm, if you can figure out that conundrum that will be the key to the mystery and you will find your answers and your investigation will be done. The search for Xavier Cockroachal Damon will be finished. Good luck."

Oh, Jesus Christ. Take Park Avenue then go to five Amsterdam Street. where there will be a hotel and use the damn key found in the locker on room number 37. You know, I really hope this person never gets a job in the intelligence community, writing secret code, because if they did, we're all totally fucked.

So, that was what the key was for. A room at the hotel on five Amsterdam Street. I realized there really was no other choice but to go check the room out. This was the final step of the investigation. There would be nothing more to do after this and I could be done with it all, so there really was no excuse not to. Besides, unlike myself, Olivia was still very enthusiastic about solving the mystery and I knew she'd be thrilled at the news and would really enjoy doing it. I took another gulp from my glass, picked up my phone and called her to tell her the news.

Olivia and I stood at five Amsterdam Street, outside the Dream Portal Hotel. I was wearing my backpack. Olivia spoke, "This is exciting. I can't wait to see what we find."

"I'm guessing a whole lot of nothing." I predicted dismissively.

She frowned at me. "You're always so quick to be a buzzkill. I really think you need to consider that we may find something truly monumental. It's the final step of the investigation. There has to be something big. Why must you always be so negative?"

"It was in my contract." I dead panned.

"You're a negative Nelly is what you are." Olivia commented.

"Hey, hold on, now I may damn well be negative but I ain't no Nelly." I protested.

Olivia had a questioning look. "But, we didn't really talk too much about the plan. To be honest, I was too excited to pay attention. But, you were saying we shouldn't just go check out the room right away."

"At first that's what I thought we'd do but then I got to thinking, someone has to be paying for the room and I would sort of like to know who that someone is before we blindly go walking in. I mean, I have no idea what is actually going on here." I reasoned.

"You think it could be some sort of trap?" she wondered with trepidation.

I considered the situation. "Could be, could be anything. I don't know. But you have to admit it's more than a little sketchy. We were sent to find a key that opened a locker with a different key that days later we found out was a hotel room key and all that time someone had to be paying for that hotel room. I really think we should learn more before we just go walking in. It's all very disconcerting and strange."

"So, what do we do? Do you want to stake out the room and see if anyone is coming or going?" she suggested.

"We could, but I first want to know the name of the person paying for the room." I declared.

"How do we find that out? I mean, a hotel isn't just going to give out the names of the guests to some random strangers." she surmised.

I knowingly smirked. "Normally, no, that would be the policy, but this is a fleabag, rundown motel, there are ways around that. Slip the person at the desk a twenty and they'll gladly tell you anything you want to know."

She looked at me with a quizzical look. "It's strange that all the messages you received were from that person who kept insisting you were in a hotel and now the final step brings us to an actual hotel."

I nodded my head. "Yes, very."

"What do you think that means?" Olivia pondered.

"I have absolutely no idea. I have no idea what any of this is about and that's why we can't let our guard down. A lot of crazy people out there, doing a lot of crazy things in this world. I have no idea what we may be walking into. Maybe we'll find Xavier Cockroachal Damon or maybe we'll find the guy who kept bringing me the telegrams, sitting in the room. I have no idea." I hypothesized, honestly having no idea what to expect.

"But, you think it could be dangerous?" Olivia asked with some alarm.

"It really could be. I never stopped to think about that as we were doing any of this or even when we found out it was a key for a hotel room, but on the way over here I started to get a bad feeling that there may be sinister intentions at play. Someone is paying for that room. Someone has been sending us all the clues leading us here. And remember the notes that kept warning us we were travelling a dangerous path, that our lives might be in danger. That is worrisome. I want to know who that someone is. What is their end game?" I expounded.

Olivia appeared visibly nervous. "Now you've got me worried."

"You should be. This may not be safe. You know, maybe we should just turn around and forget about it. I have a bad feeling." I suggested, feeling a bad premonition of what awaited us in the room.

Olivia responded with emotion, "I think we have to at least check it out. We've come this far. I can't walk away and never know what was there. I would always wonder and it would be eating away at me."

I put up my hand to try and calm her. "Look, I know you want to know, so we can check it out but just be careful and stay vigilant. I still think this might be a mistake and we should just walk away, though."

Olivia nodded her head with certainty. "I will, and if there is any sign of trouble we leave right there and then."

It was obvious this was important to her so I acquiesced. "If this is what you want to do, we'll do it."

"And we should have the person at the front desk call up to the room, see if anybody answers." she suggested.

"Yeah, that's a good idea." I agreed.

"I think we'll be fine." she announced with confidence.

"I hope so. I wouldn't want anything to happen to you. Hopefully we're not walking into the lair of some serial killer with far too much time on his hands, but I have no idea what will be waiting for us, so keep your head up, you hear me." I urged her.

Olivia nodded her head. "I will. So, should we go in?"

I looked at the entrance to the hotel. "Yeah, I guess so. Let's go find out what's going on here."

We walked into the lobby, me hobbling on my walker. It clearly was not a five star establishment. Seedy would be an appropriate word for it. We went up to the counter behind which stood a middle aged man, balding, three day stubble on his face. He looked at me and I spoke, "Excuse me, I was wondering if you could help me out. The person staying in room 37, we were talking but I've forgotten their name. Could you tell me what it is?"

"You should know I can't give out the names of any of the guests." the hotel clerk grumbled, dryly.

"Oh, no, I'm not the one asking." I replied with an attempted suave tone. I pulled out a twenty dollar bill and placed it on the counter. "It's Andrew Jackson that is asking."

The man behind the counter looked at me with an irritated sneer. "Look, don't try to be cute here. Just say I'll give you twenty bucks if you tell me who is staying in room 37 and I'll tell you. Don't try and pull that dumb shit, like this is some sort of movie, it's annoying."

"Sorry, um, then I'll give you twenty bucks if you tell me who is staying in room 37." I meekly offered.

"Deal." The man took the twenty dollar bill and put it in his pocket. "Let me look it up." The clerk opened a tall, thin logbook and began turning the pages. "Let's see, room 37, staying there is, oh boy, quite the name on this one. Staying in room 37 is a, Xavier Cockroachal Damon." Olivia and I looked at each other with surprise. "Cockroachal, well at least he chose a fitting hotel, staying in this dump."

"Thank you. Um, one more thing, could you ring up to his room?" I requested.

"Why not." The hotel clerk picked up a phone and pressed some buttons. After a while he hung up the phone. "No one is answering."

"OK, thank you for your help." I acknowledged.

"Why not, thanks for the twenty." the clerk replied then turned and walked into the room behind the counter.

I turned to Olivia to cut off what I expected her to say. "OK, look, that the person who checked into the room used the name Xavier Cockroachal Damon really doesn't mean anything. This whole thing has been about trying to find him so that they would use that name tells us absolutely nothing."

"I know, but still, I got chills when he said the name. I wasn't expecting that." she conveyed with wonderment.

"Me either, but this changes nothing. We have to stay on our toes." I cautioned.

"No one answered when he called up." Olivia commented.

"Just because no one answered, doesn't mean no one is there." I pointed out.

"Let's go check the room and see. And, who knows, maybe we will find Xavier Cockroachal Damon in the room." Olivia eagerly declared.

There was no elevator so I folded my walker and Olivia and I walked up to the third floor. I unfolded my walker when we reached it and we walked along the hall to room 37. What would be inside? We were about to find out. I used the key and opened the door. We looked into the room. It was a small room. I saw no one inside and it looked completely undisturbed.

"There's nobody here." she observed.

I scanned the room. "Doesn't appear to be. Leave the door open and you stay here, just in case. I'm going to go in and check the bathroom, the closet, anywhere else a person could be hiding. If the coast is clear then come on in."

"Let me do it." she offered.

I shook my head. "No, just in case, I don't want anything to happen to you. For now, just stay here. That way, if anything bad does go down, you can get away." I entered the room and turned on the light and looked around. I walked over to the closet and opened it. There was nothing in the closet, not a person, nor even any objects at all. I walked through the room, looking around. "Um, closet is fine, but it's strange, I don't actually see any personal effects of any kind that would show anybody is staying in this room."

"That is odd." Olivia commented with a peculiar look.

"Let me see what I find in the bathroom." I walked to the bathroom and turned on the light. There was no one in there. To be safe, I walked over and looked behind the shower curtain. Nothing. Like the outer room there was no sign anyone had been using it. In a dish by the sink there was a bar of soap, still with its plastic on, and there was a little bottle of shampoo. I picked it up. It was full. That was all there was. I walked back to the main part of the hotel room. "No one there." I called out to Olivia.

"So, can I come in now?" Olivia asked.

"Um, wait, let me just check under the bed. Who knows, wouldn't want you to fall victim to the diabolical under bed killer." I walked over to the bed. I placed my walker to the side and put my hands on the mattress and kneeled down on the floor. I looked under the bed. There was nothing at all. I called out. "Wait, yeah, there's someone under here. But apparently he died of starvation, waiting for us to get here so we're good. You can come in now." I pulled myself up and sat on the bed and took my backpack off and set it on the floor.

Olivia walked into the room and closed the door. "So there's nothing?"

"Nothing at all. No sign anywhere that a person is even staying here, just the amenities, if you even want to call them that, of a couple of unused glasses on the nightstand and unused toiletries in the bathroom.." I observed with suspicion.

"You think there'd be something." Olivia commented.

"Something, a book, a paper, some clothes." An idea occurred to me. "Wait, go over to the bureaux and see if there's anything in there. There's a drawer on the nightstand here, I'll check that."

Olivia walked over to the bureaux and opened the drawers. "There's nothing in here. Nothing at all."

I pulled open the drawer on the nightstand. "Nothing in here, either."

Olivia had a queer look. "That's strange." She walked over and sat on the bed beside me.

"I mean, if a person is staying in a hotel room, you'd think there would be some sign of it, however small." I hypothesized, perplexed.

"So, what do you make of it?" Olivia asked.

I shrugged. "I have no clue what to make of it."

"What do we do now?" she asked with puzzlement.

"I have no idea. This hasn't exactly turned into the treasure trove of answers one might have hoped for." something then dawned on me, "And, I really never thought about it until right now but a hotel like this, I'm sure they would only give out one key per room so when we found the key in the storage unit, that's the only key for the room."

"Management would have another key." Olivia mentioned.

"Sure, but why would management send us a key to one of their rooms? And someone is paying for this room, someone checked in then sent us the only key, which we had for however long without knowing what it was for and when we eventually find out, we show up and they are nowhere to be seen, even though they've been paying for the room all this time." I contemplated.

Olivia looked at me with confusion. "So, what do you think is going on?"

"I have no idea. It doesn't make any bloody sense. It hurts my head, is what it does." I pulled out a bottle of vodka from my bag. "I need a drink." I filled a glass on the nightstand and drank from it.

"You always need a drink. But, what do we do now?" Olivia asked.

"In terms of the mission, I really don't care." I drank again from my glass, "You know, it is Friday, so I say we just make it a three day weekend and enjoy the hotel room someone is paying for."

Olivia showed a curious look. "Just stay here?"

I threw my hands up in the air, you know, I really have to stop doing that, eventually it's going to cause shoulder damage. "Why not? The room is paid for. Call it an impromptu vacation. Just get away from everything, away from all the crap. Just be alone together and say to hell with the rest of the world, just be together in our own world where nothing else matters."

"But, what about finding Xavier Cockroachal Damon?" Olivia pondered.

I drank again from the glass. "I really don't even care. You know, if while we're here, he actually came knocking on the door, announcing himself, you know what I'd do, I'd say go away, we're busy, I got better things to do. And the better things I have to do is just being with you."

"You're just saying that." Olivia deflected.

I stared into her eyes and held her hand. "No, I mean it. Who gives a damn about any of the finding Xavier Cockroachal Damon nonsense. For reasons I really can't explain, it appears we've been gifted this hotel room. Um, this pretty crappy, rundown hotel room. but we're here all the same, so I say we take advantage of it."

Olivia had a peculiar look on her face. "Being in this room, does it bring back any memories?"

"What do you mean?" I asked, not understanding.

Olivia shook her head, nonchalantly. "Oh, I don't know, I guess I mean, just memories of staying in a hotel with someone."

I thought about it. "Um, I actually never have stayed in a hotel with anyone."

Olivia reacted with surprise. "Really, not ever?"

I shrugged. "No, never. But I want to just stay in this hotel room with you. Come on, let's play hooky from our lives. All I want right now is to be here with you. Go to sleep together. Wake up beside you. We'll be like a married couple away on vacation."

"Married couple. Oh, but not that you would ever possibly think of marrying lowly, little me. That's why it's just playing hooky from real life, all just pretend." Olivia summarized, sounding disappointed.

I drank again from my glass, an odd look on my face. "Um, well, look, I never thought I would ever want to marry anyone. It's just not me. I never imagined there would ever be someone I would want to be with. But, I really like being with you. The world is a less dreary, despondent, miserable shitfest of disgustitudes and inconceivable stupidity and pointless, meaningless, abhorrent, sickening, craptitude when I'm around you."

"Wow, that's some high praise." she responded, sarcastically.

"But, but, it, it is. I can't help it." I stammered. "That's the way I see life and the world. There's no way I'm ever going to wake and see it all different than the shit it is. It's not in my DNA. In truth, life, the world, I absolutely despise and hate it."

She poked me playfully with her finger. "That's because you're a gloomy Gus."

"I am a gloomy Gus." I confessed.

"You should make that your pen name." she suggested.

"Maybe I will, but what I'm trying to say is, this gloomy Gus is less Gloomy when around you, and I am extremely grateful for that. Look, I am honest. I don't bullshit. So don't let that downplay what I'm trying to say. The fact that I'm an absolutely miserable, worthless fuck should in no way take away from the sentiment I am trying but failing miserably to express. I really, really like you." I confessed with sincerity.

Olivia looked at me, discouraged. "Really, really like but don't love, do you?"

I took another drink, feeling flustered, emotion swelling up inside. "Look, I look at life, the world and I don't even know what that word means and that word has lost any possible meaning with its shameful overuse. It's just something people say and say far too often that strips it from having any possible meaning at all, so it's something I don't want to say. The word has been cheapened to a point where it is no more significant than any other random combination of four letters. I could say I qlur you or zech you or tlig you and it would all mean the same."

"So then you're saying you don't love me." There was hurt in her voice.

I felt feelings of affection rise up inside me and I blurted out, "What I'm trying to say is that I think I do."

"Then say it if you do." Olivia implored me.

"I, I, qlur you, I zech you, I tlig you. What else do you want me to say?" I clumsily announced, trying to protect myself from what I knew was true.

"I want you to say you love me." she appealed, impassioned.

I sighed, knowing I couldn't hide from the answer or pretend it was anything else. "I, I love you, OK I don't want to love anything but I do. I love you."

Olivia smiled ecstatically. "I love you, too. Thought you never would actually say it."

I took another drink and spoke contemplatively, "Well, I think all things being, you know, as they are, and me being me, that was a perfectly reasonable assumption, but, I do. I never expected any of this. When I got that telegram, whoever the hell sent it, this was the last thing I thought would happen. I never look forward to anything, I loathe every moment of every day as a dreaded curse I am forced to endure but with you, I actually look forward to there being a tomorrow, which is really, really freaky for me, so, my apologies if I'm not saying any of this right."

Olivia smiled and stroked my hair. "You're saying it fine. But, does that mean you would someday want to marry this lowly, little girl?"

I thought about the question but really didn't need to think about the answer, at all. "Yes. Yes, I would." I responded.

"Really." her face lit up exuberantly, "You mean it?"

"I do. It's crazy but I really do." I answered without hesitating. "And not just someday, as soon as possible, because I do love you, I really do. And when you love someone, you want to always be with them, for the rest of your life."

Olivia smiled gleefully. "Till death do us part."

"Yes. Till death do us part. It's so strange. All those cliche sayings, I always scoffed at them and flat out ridiculed them because I always thought it was all bullshit, but it's different when you actually feel it yourself and it is real. And, I do love you and I want to spend the rest of my life with you and I do want to marry you." I contemplated, seeing things differently than I ever had before.

"Then ask me." she enthusiastically beseeched.

I nodded my head. "OK, I will. Here goes. Um, can I skip the going down on one knee stuff? Because if I do, I may very well not be able to get back up."

"Of course." Olivia gripped my hand, "None of that stuff matters."

I looked into her eyes. "So then. Olivia, I do love you and I was hoping you would do me the honour of making me, well, OK, I'd really still be the most miserable man alive but, that's not to say of course, what I'm trying to say is." I shook my head, "Um, that was terrible. Let me start over. Olivia, I love you, and I was wondering if you would do me the honour of being my wife. Olivia, will you marry me?"

Olivia smiled ecstatically. "Of course!" She gave me a forceful hug and we kissed, "Of course, I'll marry you. You've made me so happy. I never expected this when we set out for the hotel. This is wonderful."

I meditated on the moment. "I assure you, I never expected this either, but I'm very glad it did happen."

"No regrets?" Olivia asked.

"None whatsoever. I'm looking forward to planning it all out, figuring out how we're going to do it." I responded, feeling actual enthusiasm.

"This has turned out splendidly, hasn't it?" Olivia commented with bliss.

I nodded my head honestly. "It really has. It's crazy, there I was worrying we might be walking into some dangerous trap, that something sinister or terrible might happen, expecting the worst. Instead, I'm here in this free hotel room with my wife who I'm going to spend the rest of my life with. It just goes to show, you never really know what is—" There was a knock at the door.

"Someone's at the door." Olivia commented with alarm and a very fearful look.

I looked at the door with great uneasiness, terrified of who could be on the other side, that all my worries about sinister intentions being behind everything could actually come to be and our new life together could be over before it ever began. I felt dread that the beautiful moment could be ripped away just like that. But, I also knew it could be anyone and it could be completely innocent. I steadied myself and took a drink from my glass. "Um, it could be the person who's paying for the room or someone who knows them. Or it could be nothing. But, just be ready in case anything happens. I'll go see who it is." I stood up from the bed.

"Be careful. Ask who it is first." Olivia cautioned me with concern.

"I will." I got up and apprehensively walked over to the door, not using my walker, so my steps were extremely jerky, disjointed and clumsy. I called out, hoping for the best, "Yes, who is it?"

"Why, greetings, sir. I am stopping by to see how you are enjoying our fine establishment." I recognized the voice as the man, always dressed as a bellhop, who had stopped by my apartment and delivered all the telegrams.

"It's the crazy bellhop guy." I explained to Olivia.

"That's strange." Olivia remarked with surprise.

"Yes, it is." I was very worried that his true purpose would now be revealed and that it would not be good. I opened the door with trepidation and, sure enough, standing there was the same man, dressed as he had been the other times.

"How are you today, sir? How are you enjoying your stay at our hotel?" the man cheerfully asked.

Seeing it was him in no way put my mind at ease, if anything it only increased my concern since I still had no idea what his intentions were or what the game he was playing was. "You don't remember me?" I asked with caution.

The man smiled gleefully. "Why, of course I do. You are a guest at our lovely hotel. Why, we have spoken several times before where I asked you how you were enjoying your stay and delivered telegrams that had arrived at the front desk."

I looked at him, utterly perplexed because he was the same as he had always been. I had no clue what to make of it all. "Yeah, but those other times I was actually in my apartment, not in a hotel, and now you're showing up here. As for that, all you have to do is take one look around to know this isn't the sort of place that would have a bellhop who goes to the rooms to ask how the guests are enjoying their stay, so I know full damn well you don't actually work here, either. Really, who are you?"

"Why, I am merely an employee here at our lovely hotel whose job is to see if its guests have anything I might assist them with so they better enjoy their stay." the man replied, dutifully.

"How would you know I would be here? Are you the one sending all the telegrams? Are you paying for the room? Did you send me on the quest to find Xavier Cockroachal Damon?" I confronted him, knowing I had to uncover who he actually was, get to the truth, whatever it may be.

The man looked back with a confused expression. "I assure you, I haven't a clue what you are referring to. The telegrams I merely delivered when they arrived at the front desk and I am unaware who the sender was. As for paying for the room, it is absolutely true my job is to ensure our guests best enjoy their stay here though actually paying for the room is outside my responsibilities or capabilities. And, as for enlisting you in a quest to find an Xavier Cockroachal Damon, I must say that is without a doubt the most ridiculously idiotic name I have ever heard and that cannot possibly be a real person so why anyone would send you on that errand I can in no way fathom. So, I am sorry, fine sir, but you have me at a loss."

He hadn't broken character at all for even a moment and in no way seemed a threat, just his usual cheery, congenial self. I felt completely bewildered. "Really, I see. Tell me, you wouldn't have, by any chance, received another telegram for me?"

The man smiled joyfully. "Why, indeed sir, I have. It arrived at the front desk just a few minutes ago and I was tasked with delivering it to you thusly. Here you are." The man handed me a large envelope.

I looked at the envelope in my hand. "Yes, thank you, then."

"If there is anything else I can do for you, please do not hesitate to call down to the front desk. I hope you enjoy the rest of your day." The man cheerily chimed then turned and walked away. I closed the door and walked back to the bed with the telegram and sat down.

"That was really bizarre." Olivia remarked.

"That, indeed it was. And I really need another drink." I awkwardly stumbled back towards the bed.

"Be careful." Olivia cautioned, nervously.

I reached the bed and sat down. I filled my glass from my bottle and drank.

"Open the telegram. We have to see what it says." Olivia announced, excitedly.

I ripped open the envelope. What was written was very brief. I read it out loud, "Congratulations. You found your answer." I looked at the telegram with a puzzled look, "That's it. That's all it says. Nothing else. What does this mean?"

"Congratulations. You found your answer. It really doesn't say anything else?" Olivia asked, confused.

"Nothing. Here, read for yourself." I handed the message to her and she read it.

Olivia nodded her head. "I see." She set the paper with the message on it down on the bed.

I drank again from my glass. "But, what does it mean? We didn't find any answer about where Xavier Cockroachal Damon is, only that someone is paying for this hotel room under that name and, that someone isn't here. And to arrive at the moment it did? Is it saying you are my answer? How could whoever wrote the message know that? What exactly is this all about? What is going on here? My God, my head is spinning. And my forever cure for my head spinning is to have more drinks and another cigarette. None of this makes any sense." I pulled out and lit a cigarette and drank again from the glass.

Olivia got an introspective look. "Maybe it all makes perfect sense, just not in the way you expected."

I took a drag from my cigarette and looked at Olivia, flabbergasted. "But it doesn't make any sense. The bellhop, the telegrams, leading me to you. I mean, what, was the bellhop playing matchmaker under the guise of a search to find Xavier Cockroachal Damon?"

"Would you be glad if that was it?" Olivia asked, thoughtfully.

I took another long drag from my cigarette. "Well, yes, and thankful for it. But that doesn't mean it makes any sense."

She shrugged then spoke with a meditative tone, "Maybe it's not supposed to. Maybe there are things that happen that can't be explained. Maybe we just accept them and don't question. You say it doesn't make any sense but when is it, life ever does? Maybe sometimes things do just happen for a reason. Maybe we should just enjoy the room as the first vacation of a married couple. Maybe that is the answer."

I just looked into her eyes. I took another drag from my cigarette then put it out in an ashtray on the nightstand. "I think you're right, my wife. Look, none of this has made any sense and it all has really hurt my head. But, you know, I really don't care. I cannot fathom what the hell was going on here, but it doesn't even matter. It brought me to you and that's all that matters."

"And you really do want to marry me?" Olivia asked, appearing anxious to do so.

I nodded my head with a loving look. "I really do. So, to hell with everything else. I just want to enjoy this room with my wife."

She smiled ecstatically. "You have no idea how good that makes me feel. I was wondering, would it be OK if you poured me a glass?"

"But, you've said you never drink." I commented.

"I don't, but you just proposed to me and I gladly accepted so we're going to be married. It's a special occasion, a celebration. Just a little bit is all." she smiled gleefully.

"No problem then if that's what you want." I poured some of the vodka into the other glass on the nightstand. "It is a celebration, so, certainly, I shall pour me lady a glass." I handed the glass to her.

"Thank you." She sipped from the glass and I drank from mine. "It is wonderful, isn't it?"

I thought about it all, all that had transpired. "It really is."

"I say this moment calls for a toast." Olivia announced, raising her glass.

"Indeed, it does." I raised my glass as well, "So then, a toast to the first day of the rest of our lives."

Olivia smiled contentedly and euphorically. "A toast to the first day of the rest of our lives."

We clanged our glasses together, then we each took a sip then set the glasses down on the nightstand and looked into each other's eyes. We shared a long, deep kiss, having officially entered into the first day of the rest of our new lives.

So, that's the story, and it really was a crazy chain of events. I, Aaron Aaronson, was in love and I was actually looking forward to the future and I was going to get married. Nothing could be crazier than that. I had been writing the story as events unfolded because they had sparked something in me. I had no idea where it would all lead but I wanted to document it, and as my relationship with Olivia grew, I knew it was a story I wanted to tell. The block of seeming meaningless nothing was shattered by what I was feeling. I write this now as Olivia is in the bathroom, taking a shower. When she went in, I took my laptop from my bag and continued the story I was writing because I truly was inspired to detail all that had transpired since we left for the hotel. All of it truly was inspirational and I wanted to capture it in the moment, hopefully before waking and finding it was all a dream and I had just been returned to the dismal, despair and degradation of life as I had known it up to this moment. It always seemed I had been condemned to the life I had known and that anything good was never to be afforded to me. I had actually given up on life long ago. It was just an empty, pointless, dreary slog of steps leading nowhere. Nothing ever seemed to work out for me and I was certain they never would. I now realized that no matter how bleak or futile life may seem, you never can truly give up because you never know what will happen or what the future will bring. I mocked and ridiculed the notion of hope because what did it ever bring but disappointment and despair. In this moment, I understood that no matter how bad things are, no matter how down and defeated you are, somewhere inside you do have to keep that sliver of hope alive, even if hidden away to shield yourself from the failures at realizing it. Because, if you don't, the greatest thing ever in your life could stand right there before you and you wouldn't even be able to see it and it will pass you by and be lost forever. I suppose that is the real lesson of this story. I guess, in truth, I hadn't actually totally given up. I just turned away from the idea of hope. Inside, I guess I did still have dreams of a better life and a better tomorrow, regardless of how foolish they seemed. I'm glad for that, because no matter what, you have to have hope. Without that, life truly is nothing. And now, my life was going to be so much more than I ever imagined it could be. I honestly did feel like the luckiest guy in the world, and lucky, well that was something that this guy never actually was. Anyway, I just heard the water turn off. She will be out shortly so I'm going to end the story here. It is indeed time to begin the first day of the rest of my life, a life I actually am looking forward to, rather than only wishing it to end, which was what I had always wanted before now. I'm glad there will be a tomorrow. Everything I had ever thought about life was different now. I was actually optimistic about the future. That statement absolutely seems impossible to be believed considering my feelings and thoughts about life up to this point, but, as the old adage goes, truth indeed can be stranger than fiction.

The End

ADDENDUM: WRITTEN BY MARK COMSTOCK

The story doesn't actually end there, though. There is still more of the story to tell. I will be the one to take over responsibility for telling it, rather than Aaron Aaronson.

Olivia stood in front of her phone that was set up over by the table in the hotel room and was recording video.

"Um, are we like recording a sex video here?" Aaron Aaronson asked, curiously.

The recording camera of the phone was blocked by Olivia as she tried to position it on the table. "No, we're not recording a sex video, you dirty boy. I wouldn't want to do that. What if someone else ever saw it? I'd be mortified."

"Then what is it exactly we're doing here?" Aaron Aaronson inquired.

"Just recording the first moments of the start of our life together, for posterity." Olivia answered.

"You know, I'm shy having my picture taken or being recorded so I'll probably just have my hand in front of my face the whole time we're talking." Aaron Aaronson remarked, taking a drink.

Olivia made a dismissive hand gesture. "Don't be silly, you have a beautiful face. This is us starting our life together. I want to record it so we can look back on it, years from now. Come on, let me do this."

"I didn't say you couldn't do it. I just said I'd probably have my hand over my face the whole time." Aaron Aaronson explained.

Olivia walked away from the phone and got on the bed next to Aaron Aaronson, the both of them leaning back against the pillows, both visible in the recording video. "Just pretend you're not actually being recorded. Come on this will be fun." Aaron Aaronson put his hand up, blocking his face and Olivia pulled it away. "Come on, stop. Just act natural."

"Yeah, well that's a little hard to do. I need another drink." Aaron Aaronson filled his glass and drank.

"Pour me some more, too." Olivia held out her glass.

"Sure." Aaron Aaronson took her glass and poured some more into it then handed it to her. "Here you go. So." He looked visibly uncomfortable, "How bout those Jets?"

"Stop it. You're ruining this." Olivia complained. "I just want to record us together, saying whatever we would be saying in this moment if the camera wasn't on, not talking for the camera."

Aaron Aaronson shook his head, playfully mockingly then took a drink. "Then you probably shouldn't have told me you were putting the camera on because now I can't stop thinking that there is a camera recording me and natural is a state that is an impossibility."

"Oh, geez, this is going horribly." Olivia drank from her glass.

"I'm afraid it does not bode well for our marriage." Aaron Aaronson commented.

Olivia slapped him lightly on the shoulder. "Don't say that. We're going to have a great marriage."

"Yes, I know we will." Aaron Aaronson concurred.

Olivia nodded her head once with a look of satisfaction. "That's better. You better not ever think about divorcing me or being with someone else." Olivia took a drink then held out her glass, "Pour me a little more, will you?"

"Really, more? Well, sure." Aaron Aaronson poured a little more into her glass.

"I always dreamed of one day getting married and now it's actually happening." Olivia declared with a dreamy look on her face.

Aaron Aaronson drank from his glass. "I never thought I'd ever get married. I never saw that happening."

The look on Olivia's face became peculiar, distracted. She drank from her glass. "Really, you never thought you would ever get married?"

"Never. I never thought that would happen." Aaron Aaronson declared.

"Not ever?" Olivia asked.

Aaron Aaronson shook his head. "No."

Olivia drank again from her glass and spoke with a more rigid sounding voice, "Really? You mean though, you never thought you would ever get married again."

"What do you mean?" Aaron Aaronson asked, appearing confused.

Olivia's face seemed troubled. "I'm just saying that when you say you never thought you would get married, what you mean to say is you never thought you would get married again."

Aaron Aaronson looked at Olivia, scrunching his face, "You have me confused here. What are you saying?"

Olivia spoke with apparent concern in her voice. "I'm just saying that when you say you never thought that you'd get married, how can that be true when you've been married before?"

Aaron Aaronson appeared even more baffled. "What? I've never been married."

"Really, are you sure about that?" Olivia asked with a cutting tone.

"Yes, I'm sure about that." Aaron Aaronson declared, seeming exasperated. He drank from his glass. "I think I would sort of know if I had been. What's going on. What's gotten into you?"

The look on Olivia's face turned uneasy and she spoke apologetically, "Oh, I'm sorry. Must be the drinking. I really never do so I guess it's hitting me funny."

Aaron Aaronson put his hand on her shoulder and spoke reassuringly, "It's OK, it's fine. But, don't worry, I have never been married. This is my first time and I'm really looking forward to it."

Olivia's expression was troubled. "Don't worry. Yes, of course, don't worry. Just don't worry. Why worry?" Olivia barked the words dramatically in seeming distress then she drank the rest of the vodka that was in her glass. She held out her empty glass. "Can I have another?"

Aaron Aaronson looked at her with a look of concern. "You sure you should? I think maybe you should stop."

"Oh, this from the person who drinks his weight in liquor on a daily basis." she taunted. "Come on, just one more, it's a celebration, after all. Please. I'll be good, I promise."

"OK, if you want it. Admittedly, I wouldn't be the ideal spokesperson for moderation. Here you go." Aaron Aaronson poured some more into her glass.

"Thank you. Of course, I say I'll be good, but, later, I could be a bad girl if you wanted." Olivia invited with a seductive tone, stroking his hair.

Aaron Aaronson nodded approvingly. "That sounds good, yes."

Olivia stared ahead at the recording phone with a reflective, wistful look. "You know, I actually used to drink but I stopped. Maybe it was a mistake having these drinks. I can lose control and become a different person. I stopped because I didn't like that person. I wanted to celebrate, but doing it this one time is it for me." She drank from her glass.

Aaron Aaronson drank from his glass. "That's fine. It's good you see that. Why don't we do a second recording tomorrow, without the drinks, a do over."

"You'll be drinking though, of course." Olivia commented with a smirk.

"Of course. You know it's not for you and you don't want to do it. I know it is for me and I'll stop doing it when I'm six feet under. Only then because I plan to have a few farewell shots when I'm still on the slab." Aaron Aaronson drank from his glass.

Olivia looked at Aaron Aaronson with an astonished look. "Wow, how you drink. It's amazing the amount you drink. And it really doesn't change you at all."

"Actually, it does, it gets me drunk." Aaron Aaronson deadpanned, then took a drink.

Olivia drank again from her glass then spoke, reflective, "Me, I do become a different person, but you already knew that."

"Yes, because you just told me." Aaron Aaronson replied.

Olivia exhaled, seeming aggravated. "No, I meant from before."

"Before?" Aaron Aaronson asked, seeming very confused.

"Yes, before." Olivia snapped, looking very agitated then drank from her glass.

Aaron Aaronson looked at her with a baffled look. "What are you saying? Before what?"

"Before now!" Olivia shouted.

"OK, you are really confusing the hell out of me here. You're not making any sense." Aaron Aaronson protested with alarm.

Olivia shot back with a venom in her voice, "I'm not making any sense? You're the one that isn't making any sense when you say you don't know what I mean when I say before now!"

"What are you saying? I can't understand any of it." Aaron Aaronson pleaded, exasperated.

Olivia looked at him with a caustic look of scorn. She drank from her glass. "Oh, God, do you know how insulting that is? How that makes me feel? How it hurts?"

"What is wrong with you? Really, what are you saying?" Aaron Aaronson pleaded.

Olivia looked him straight in the eyes and said, "The times *before now*, when we would lie in this very same room and drink together and make love and be together. I actually liked lying here, drinking with you, but after you left me, I quit. I stopped."

Aaron Aaronson had a look of bewilderment on his face. "What the hell are you talking about? You're really scaring me here."

Olivia shook her head, incredulous. "God, I thought if I brought us back here you would remember, but, still, even now, you really don't remember anything at all?"

Aaron Aaronson was looking very flustered and panicked. "No, I don't. Are you telling me we have been in this room together before? That's impossible. I would actually remember that. There may be things I can't remember when I drink but I know I would remember that. I think the alcohol is making you crazy because I am absolutely certain I have never been with you in this room before today. That's crazy."

Olivia gave a coy look. "Well. I suppose in a sense that is actually true. I was never in this room before with Aaron Aaronson."

"Exactly. So what are you talking about?" Aaron Aaronson exclaimed, obviously very upset.

Olivia nodded her head then drank from her glass, finishing what was in it, then setting it down on the bed. She spoke with a peculiar tone, "No. But, I did share many days and nights in this room with Xavier Cockroachal Damon."

The look on Aaron Aaronson's face was of complete shock. "What? Why would you. why would you tell me that? What are you? You are *really* scaring me here."

Olivia looked at Aaron Aaronson inquisitively. "You've never told me before, what happened? How did you wind up on the walker?"

"I, I, don't really know. My mind was crazy around that time. I, I can't really remember." Aaron Aaronson stammered, disoriented, then drank from his glass.

Olivia looked at Aaron Aaronson with a severe stare. "You didn't die when you went over that waterfall, fighting Moriarty. You were found on the shore a few days later. No, you didn't die from the fall but it did cripple you and you lost your memory."

The look on Aaron Aaronson's face was of pure horror. "What? Wait, are you trying to say? Are you trying to say—"

"You *are* Xavier Cockroachal Damon." Olivia vehemently declared.

"That's insane! That's not possible." Aaron Aaronson replied with disbelief, shaking his head.

"Really?" Olivia looked at him with a pointed stare, "You say you can't remember when you became crippled but, tell me, what about before that? What do you remember from then?"

Aaron Aaronson appeared discombobulated and he held his palm to his forehead. "Um, I, I don't know, my mind was, I, I don't know."

"Do you remember anything?" Olivia asked, probingly.

"Um, I, no, I guess. I never really gave it any thought. I remember waking up and I was crippled and I just went on from there." Aaron Aaronson exclaimed, obviously befuddled.

Olivia gave a look of consternation. "And you don't think that's odd?"

Aaron Aaronson appeared very flustered and anxious. "I don't know. I just, I just never thought about it. I just went on."

Olivia raised her voice forcefully, "You don't remember because there was no Aaron Aaronson before then. Before then there was Xavier Cockroachal Damon!"

"Wait, you are coming at me with a lot of crazy stuff here." Aaron Aaronson refilled his glass and drank, "How am I supposed to believe any of this is true? It can't be. And wait, so then, all the, all the telegrams, the clues, the bellhop, the keys, all of that was your doing?"

"Yes." Olivia simply replied.

Aaron Aaronson looked at her, a look of realization on his face. "The key, this room, so you're the one paying for it?"

"Yes." she simply replied.

"Why?" Aaron Aaronson asked, bewildered.

"Well, you were the one who paid the other times we were here so it only seemed fair that this time was on me." Olivia glibly retorted.

"But, why, why did you do all of it?" Aaron Aaronson pressed.

"Because I wanted you to come to this room and find Xavier Cockroachal Damon." Olivia spoke with profound purpose.

"I'm Xavier Cockroachal Damon?" Aaron Aaronson asked, astonished.

Olivia nodded her head. "Yes, you are."

"And we were together in this room?" Aaron Aaronson asked with disbelief.

"We were together in this room, in every way." Olivia replied with a sultry, provocative voice.

"But, but I've read Xavier Cockroachal Damon's autobiography. I don't remember you ever being mentioned." Aaron Aarobson pointed out.

Olivia's look became one of pure resentment and bitter scorn. She slammed her hand down on the mattress, knocking her glass over the side of the bed to the floor. "Oh, thrust the knife into my heart. I tell you how much all of this hurts me, how horrible it makes me feel and what do you do? Throw it in my face that you never mentioned me, at all. Never wrote a single story about me, did you? Well, you certainly couldn't stop writing about her, could you, your bitch wife? But where was she when we were together and I would watch you cry that she was the only woman you ever loved and, still she was rejecting you, wouldn't take your hand. I was there for you every moment. I loved you from the start. She treated you like crap and wanted nothing to do with you. We were here together, but, still, all you could think about was her, all you wanted was her even though I was here for you. And we would just be together, make love, then spend the day intertwined, and we would lay there and drink and talk, me lying there naked, except for the rose petals you would sometimes cover my body with. We were in love."

"Rose petals?" Aaron Aaronson mumbled, looking unnerved.

Olivia's expression became very angry. "But then she has a change of heart and you walk away from me and leave me, cold and alone, and then you marry her. I should have been the one you married. I gave you all of myself, completely, and you just discarded me like a piece of trash. That's why I wanted to take a shower, to see if I could wash the filth off this dirty, worthless whore. Because, in the end you loved her, only her, and I was just a meaningless nothing you used and who you liked to fuck. I loved you. You should have loved me. I should have been the one you married."

Aaron Aaronson got a more uneasy look. "Wait. Your mom said something about a time when someone really hurt you but she never knew who the person was."

"It was you!" Olivia screamed.

"It was me?" Aaron Aaronson asked, looking pale.

"You broke my heart." Olivia declared with anguish.

Aaron Aaronson shook his head, looking astonished, then drank from his glass. "I'm very sorry, but I don't, I don't remember any of it."

Olivia's expression sharpened into a hateful scowl. "You don't even remember *her*?"

Aaron Aaronson shook his head. "No."

"How about your daughter? You weren't the biological father, of course, but she definitely was your daughter." Olivia pressed.

"I don't remember anything. I remember nothing." Aaron Aaronson proclaimed with an astonished look of distress.

Olivia spoke contemplatively, "You know, I actually think that somewhere in your mind you still do. Remember, the first telegram started by mentioning Hurphuldurp Mahangahoo and how he may actually be Xavier Cockroachal Damon. Hurphuldurp Mahangahoo was never a real person. One reads the story and one would very well think it was just the three of you wearing ridiculous disguises but none of it was real. The story was actually written by you in a drunken fever dream. It was you remembering them and dreaming of being with them. You knew yourself then as Aaron Aaronson but you attached a different pen name. Do you really not remember writing that?"

"No, I don't. I actually wrote that story?" Aaron Aaronson asked.

"You did." Olivia let out a sharp, piercing laugh, "And oh, what a surprise, I didn't appear anywhere in that story, either. You, dreaming of the life you had with her, years after you lost your memory and became Aaron Aaronson. Even then, it's still all about her, never me. It's her. Only her. And, wow, I never even appeared in The Missing Years. I suppose you get a pass for that one because we hadn't actually met, yet. But, the thing of it is, in it you did tell stories of other women you were with, yet, never a single story or even a single mention of me in anything, not ever, not one single word. Though, after we were together, so many about *her*." Olivia's expression became very angry and hurt, "Well, if somewhere in that brain you can still remember her then somewhere in that brain I want you to remember me. I want you to remember *me*!"

The look on Aaron Aaronson's face was pained. "I can't remember any of it! I don't, I don't remember!"

"Try!" Olivia shouted.

"I can't!" Aaron Aaronson shouted back.

Olivia's voice became louder and more commanding, "Try harder! Look inside! Remember all you know about Xavier Cockroachal Damon and know that that was you. I want you to remember! I want you to see *me!*"

Aaron Aaronson shook his head with distress. "I can't! I can't remember any of it!"

Olivia pointed forcefully at him. "Yes, you can! Focus inside! Remember who you are!"

Aaron Aaronson shook his head and drank from his glass. "I don't care about any of that. Maybe that's what was but I don't care about any of that. I don't care about them. I don't know them. I love you. I want to marry you. I want to have a life with you. Forget about the past. It doesn't matter to me. You matter to me."

"But, you have to remember and when you do, I want you to remember me. I need you to see *me*." Olivia beseeched with longing.

"I'm very sorry if this is true and I hurt you but I can't remember any of it. This is a new day, our new day, why don't we just focus on that?" Aaron Aaronson's voice sounded mournful and sincere.

"Because, I need you to remember me." Her voice cracked with emotion. "What you have to do is focus inside, look deep in your mind, beyond what you remember. I know those memories are still in there somewhere. Look into the deepest hidden places of your mind. You can find me! You can see me. Please do that, for me."

"Look, I'll, I'll try. I'll try for you." His words sounded with sorrow. Aaron Aaronson took a drink from his glass and set it on the nightstand. He closed his eyes and put his palms on either side of his head, taking on a look of extreme concentration and distress.

"What do you see?" Olivia asked.

Aaron Aaronson shook his head and opened his eyes, speaking with frustration. "Nothing. I see nothing."

"Keep trying. I'm sure you'll find it eventually, now that you know what you're looking for." Olivia prodded.

Aaron Aaronson stood from the bed with a frustrated and confused look then dropped back down on the bed. "This is pointless. It's no use. It's not working. Just forget about this. Leave it alone."

"Come on. They're your memories. It's *your* life!" Olivia blared at him.

Aaron Aaronson spoke with malaise, "And what, all I have to do is try and remember and they'll all just come flooding back, just like that? I really don't think it works that way."

"They're still there. You can remember." Olivia implored him.

Aaron Aaronson picked up his glass and drank from it. "That is if any of this is even true. You know you started acting very bizarre so how do I know you're not just making all of this up?"

Olivia spoke with a tone of certitude, "Deep down inside, you know I'm telling the truth."

"But it's all so damn crazy!" Aaron Aaronson shouted out.

"Life is crazy." Olivia proclaimed.

"And, and, I just say, if, I have to say, if," Aaron Aaronson stammered, "if I'm actually Xavier Cockroachal Damon and I'm also the person you were so broken up about, I'm sorry but your mom is without a doubt the worst damn psychic in the history of the world. Just saying is all." he drank from his glass.

Olivia gave Aaron Aaronson an indignant glare. "Don't try to deflect with jokes. I think you're getting close. Don't be afraid. Just break through the wall and you will see."

Aaron Aaronson let out a groan of frustration then drank what was left in his glass and set it on the nightstand. He gripped his head with his hands, closing his eyes, looking even more tormented. His expression twisted even more with distress as he held his head. Then, after a few moments he pulled his hands away and opened his eyes. He had a look of absolute shock and dismay on his face. "Oh, my God. I remember standing in the water atop the waterfall."

Olivia smiled triumphantly. "Good. What else do you see?"

"Everything. I remember it all. I am Xavier Cockroachal Damon." Aaron Aaronson stood up from the bed and immediately dropped right back down upon it with a devastated look. "I can't believe it. This is too much to handle. I *really* need a drink." He filled his glass with vodka and drank it down then refilled it and sipped from it.

"And do you see me? Do you see us together in this room?" Olivia pressed.

Aaron Aaronson sipped from his glass and had a look of anguish. "I do. I see all of it. You were great to me. But, I was so caught up thinking of her, I didn't appreciate you. That wasn't fair to you. I was wrong for that. That was terrible of me."

"And, so you understand why I was so hurt?" Olivia asked, starting to tear up.

"I do. I'm sorry." Aaron Aaronson began to tear up as well. He drank from his glass. "I didn't mean to hurt you though. I was selfish. I never stopped to think about your feelings. I was so wrapped up in myself. You deserved better. I'm so sorry."

Olivia sighed, looking relieved. "And so, now that you know the full story, the truth, as we start the first day of the rest of our life together, you actually see me and can marry me as you should have done then, because I was always the one you were meant to be with. And now you realize that."

Aaron Aaronson looked at Olivia with a frozen, tormented expression. "But, she's my wife."

"What?!" Olivia screamed and jumped up from the bed.

Aaron Aaronson looked very sad and apologetic. "She's, she's my wife, don't you understand?"

"Are you fuckin kidding me?!" Olivia roared with anger.

"Don't you see? I never chose to leave her. I never wanted to. All this time, she's thought I was dead. We had a life together. I never meant to leave that life. I have to go find them. I have to let them know I'm OK" Aaron Aaronson pleaded with her.

Olivia looked at him with contempt. "Unbelievable. You're still thinking of *her*!"

Aaron Aaronson set his glass on the nightstand and stood from the bed, shouting back, overwhelmed by emotion, "What did you expect?! I didn't choose to forget her and now, just like that, every moment of my time with her fills up inside of me as though I never left her, as though it's the moment right after standing there in the water atop that waterfall. What am I supposed to do?"

"I wanted you to remember so you would see *me*!" Olivia snarled.

"But if I can see you how can I not also see her! And my daughter! My God, she must be getting big by now. I wonder how she's been. Dear God." Aaron Aaronson picked up his glass and drank what was left in it while standing, then he set the glass back on the nightstand. "And how can I not see our life together that I never wanted to leave. I am so confused and terrified right now." Aaron Aaronson stumbled, struggling to maintain his footing. He grabbed his forehead, grimacing. "I feel like I just want to explode. But I know I have to go find them. I don't have any other choice." He shook his head, looking at Olivia with despair.

Olivia stared at him, a sharpened scowl on her face. "You could choose me and stay with me and forget about her."

Aaron Aaronson reacted with a tortured desperation, stumbling again but managing to keep his balance. "How?! I am right there and I was going to go home and be with her. This is the very next moment to me. How can I just forget about all that and cast them aside as though they were never actually there, like they never existed, like they never mattered at all to me. They do matter. I love them. She was my wife. No, she is my wife."

Olivia shook her head scornfully and chuckled with disdain. "Oh. So that's how it is, then. I guess I'm just the same fool I always was, thinking you would ever choose lowly, ugly, worthless me over her. Yes, suppose I forgot the role it is for me to play, just the nasty whore you use and fuck, whereas she is your supposed soulmate, your," Olivia sneered with a mocking, hateful look, "*beauty dove.* And she is the one you love. You never will love me, will you?"

"I do love you. I really do. I wish you could understand what I'm saying." Aaron Aaronson appealed to her sorrowfully, stumbling again.

Olivia smiled sharply. "Oh, I do understand. Now you see everything. It's all clear to you. Well, I see everything clearly now, as well."

Aaron Aaronson looked at Olivia with anguish. "I love you."

Olivia shook her head with an incredulous look. "No. You don't. You never will. Because when all was said and done, I'm the one who never existed to you and I never mattered at all to you or meant a thing. You will always love her, never me." Olivias's eyes sharpened as she stared at Aaron Aaronson with a resentful scowl. She reached into her jacket pocket and pulled out a gun. She pointed it at him. Aaron Aaronson just looked back into her eyes, steadying himself on his feet. Many seconds passed, the two of them just looking into each other's eyes. Then Olivia pulled the trigger, then again and again. All three shots hit Aaron Aaronson in the chest, blood erupting as he fell to the floor. The blood flowed out and covered the floor around him. Olivia stood there, looking down with a barren expression at Aaron Aaronson's lifeless body on the floor. She placed the barrel of the gun to her chest. She pulled the trigger. Another shot rang out as she dropped to the floor. Olivia's blood flowed out across the floor, slowly creeping, inching toward the blood pool that had spilled from Aaron Aaronson, which itself was slowly inching across the floor within the silent and otherwise still room. The two blood waves connected, blending into each other, joined in union as one. So, maybe Aaron Aaronson and Olivia would not be together in life, but they would be together forever in death.

That then is the full story. As I said, there really was more to be told. I suppose the ending really wasn't quite the uplifting finale it originally seemed to be. I guess that would actually be fitting, because if you asked Aaron Aaronson what his thoughts would be on the matter he most certainly would have simply stated, "I don't believe in happy endings". So, as said, fitting, yet completely tragic that things ended as they did.

At this point, I would like to clarify how it is I am writing this. I actually knew Aaron Aaronson, not well, we weren't close friends or anything, which shouldn't come as too much of a surprise since he was a very reclusive and antisocial person. When the shots were heard, the police arrived on the scene. The bodies were taken away and they recovered Aaron Aaronson's laptop and Olivia's phone which had recorded all that had happened in the hotel room when they laid down upon the bed to commemorate the start of their life together. I actually, in passing, also knew one of the investigators of the crime scene. He was aware that I knew Aaron Aaronson and also that I, myself was a writer. Certainly, it was against regulations and was something he was not supposed to do, but after seeing the video on the phone and discovering the file of the story Aaron Aaronson was writing, he was struck by and deeply affected by how quickly everything had changed.

He made copies of both and sent them to me, feeling the full story should be told.

I confess to feeling great unease at the idea of finishing the story. They were his words. These were his events that led to the tragic end of his life. The prospect of finishing the story made me feel like a ghoul picking at his corpse and I did not like the thought of that, at all. Originally, I was not going to do it, feeling it would violate his memory and be disrespectful. But then, the more I thought about it, I came to realize that this is what he would have wanted. Aaron always believed no story was ever finished until it reached the true end. Having the story incomplete as it was would bother him greatly and I imagine, if he knew it was left in an unfinished state, he would find a way to somehow rise from the grave and finish writing it himself, alone again in a world he always despised and never wanted to be in, with this new painful memory to torment him, the cruel irony that the moment he wanted to live, it was all taken away, and he would then have to live with the pain of knowing that until again he returned to the grave. Well, no need for that second bitter end. I have completed the story as I know you would have wanted. I do it to honor your memory and your life. Now, you may rest in peace, I hope.

In the end, I know I made the right choice to finish the story. How quickly everything turned in one moment, how different everything became, truly was striking. To see a moment of true happiness and to have it so monstrously ripped apart was a part of the story that had to be told. And now it has been. And now there is nothing more to say. And so this brings to an end all words that were said, for Aaron Aaronson is dead. Um, and so brings to an end all words that were said for Xavier Cockroachal Damon is finally, actually and truly dead. Wait, what about Hurphuldurp Mahangahoo? I realize he was not actually a real person but Aaron Aaronson did begin the story relaying he received a telegram asking if Hurphuldurp Mahangahoo was actually dead so I kind of have to include him, too. Very well then. So brings to an end all words that were said for Xavier Cockroachal Damon, Aaron Aaronson, and Hurphuldurp Mahangahoo are all now dead.

In closing, it was a tragic tale where it always seemed there were more questions than answers. Unfortunately, all questions did get resolved, just not in the way one would have hoped, all questions having found their final end. Indeed, there would be no happy endings for this story. And so, what am I going to do, now that I have completed the writing of the end of the story? Well, it indeed was a very upsetting and traumatic turn of events and I need to reflect upon it and process all that happened. To see a life that always only ever wished its end, finding a moment where it truly did want to live, to then have everything so horribly torn to shreds, it really makes you think, and really strikes a bitter chord and truly is a tragic end. As I said, I need some time to try and make sense of it all. That is, if sense can even be made of it all. So what are my plans? I don't know. I guess just go out and get *really* fuckin drunk.

The End

Also by Aaron Aaronson

John Harm, Private Detective. The Case of the Evil, Global, Shadow Conspiracy: Also includes Disgusticon the Transformer and The Heist of the Century + Bonus Track!
Welcome to Nowhereland (5 Stories)
The Adventures of Man-Man, Defender of Man: (Episodes 1-10)
Self-extermination. Sounds Like a Plan: Also Includes Give Me a Burger and Hold the Fries and Brain Circus and (3 Essays About Donald J. Trump) and Man-Man, Episode 1 and Soliloquy to My Soul
Postcards from the Wasteland
Where in the World is Xavier Cockroachal Damon?

Watch for more at https://www.wastelandvoid.com.

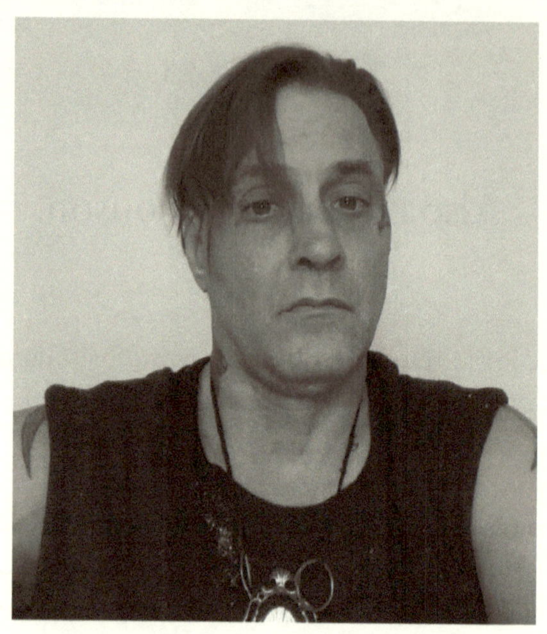

About the Author

I have written sixteen books, six under the name, Xavier Cockroachal Damon, six under the name, Aaron Aaronson, and four under the name, Mark Comstock. The books consist of novels and collections of stories and all have a lot of dark humor, often very dark. The books could be considered bizarre, outrageous, absurd and audacious. They are uncompromising, unconventional, irreverent and, most definitely, off the beaten path.

Read more at https://www.wastelandvoid.com.